Love Takes Flight

D1024225

Love Takes Flight

℘

Jane Peart

Fleming H. Revell
A Division of Baker Book House Co
Grand Rapids, Michigan 49516

© 1984, 1994 by Jane Peart

Published by Fleming H. Revell
a division of Baker Book House Company
P.O. Box 6287, Grand Rapids, MI 49516-6287

First published by Thomas Nelson, Inc.
Printed in the United States of America

All rights reserved. No part of this publication may be reproduced, stored in a retrieval system, or transmitted in any form or by any means—electronic, mechanical, photocopy, recording, or any other—without the prior written permission of the publisher. The only exception is brief quotations in printed reviews.

Scripture quotations are from The New King James Version. Copyright © 1979, 1980, 1982, Thomas Nelson, Inc., Publishers.

Library of Congress Cataloging-in-Publication Data

Peart, Jane.
    Love takes flight / Jane Peart.
      p.   cm.
        ISBN 0-8007-5513-8
      I. Title.
PS3566.E238L68   1994
813'.54—dc20   94-587

All of the characters and events in this book are fictitious. Any resemblance to actual persons, living or dead, or to actual events is purely coincidental.

To the two Saras, Ashcraft and Parsons,
With love and appreciation

Chapter One

"Two more hours' delay!" Roblynn Mallory exclaimed in dismay. That meant she had no chance of making it back to Atlanta in time for her roommate Cindy's kitchen shower. In fact, if her flight had any further rescheduling, she might not even make it back for the wedding on Saturday!

"Sorry!" The Operations agent at Chicago's O'Hare Airport shook his head sympathetically as the pretty Trans-Continent stewardess sighed in frustration. "We will be issuing another EDT in about an hour when the weather report comes down," he told her as she turned away.

"Thanks," Robbie said, smiling ruefully. "I know this fog is not your fault, Tim." She started across the crowded terminal lobby toward the crew lounge in search of Jean Ames, her fellow flight attendant, to relay this latest information.

Robbie was unaware of the many admiring glances following her as she passed. Although she could not be called beautiful, she had an indefinable quality that always commanded second looks. There was a vitality in her graceful walk, in the way she held her head, and in her slender figure clad in the distinctive, designer-created blue uniform. Besides her clear, lovely skin, she had a radiant smile and unusual golden-hazel eyes. Most important of all, Robbie had that glowing "All-American Girl" look, which was exactly the image Trans-Con wanted to project.

At the door of the lounge, Robbie paused and scanned the room for Jean. At least nine crews from various other flights stranded by weather were sitting around, drinking coffee, swapping horror stories of grounded flights, and complaining of the havoc done to personal plans.

Not spotting Jean in the crowded room, Robbie decided to wait for her a while before looking elsewhere. As she stood there she became aware of a steady appraising gaze and immediately felt her face get warm.

Robbie, who had a tendency to blush and hated it, turned away annoyed. She was not averse to male attention, but from this particular source it was unwelcome.

Robbie had recognized him on sight. What Trans-Con "stew" wouldn't? The notorious Captain T. J. Lang looked exactly the way a dashing airline pilot is supposed to look but seldom does. He also was considered to be the most eligible, least obtainable bachelor in the whole Trans-Con fleet of pilots, and rumored to collect girlfriends as some people collect matchbooks and to discard them just as casually.

Robbie ignored the frankly admiring look directed at her and walked over to the coffee machine. Men like T. J. Lang irritated Robbie. They were always trying to live up to their reputations and never missed an opportunity to make an impression on any available girl. Robbie lifted her chin in what she hoped was an aloof manner. She was not interested in giving the cool captain a chance to while away some time because he was bored.

Like all stewardesses Robbie had grown accustomed to the evaluating stares of passengers, but she resented

Captain Lang's unabashed appraisal. She had encountered his type often on flight and had developed an inner resistance to that kind of easy charm. A man like T. J. Lang was not in Robbie's game plan for life.

Robbie took off her jaunty blue cap, tucked it into the flap of her carry-on bag, and carelessly ruffled her casually styled, russet-brown hair. She got a Styrofoam cup from the stack beside the dispenser, filled it with coffee, and took it over to one of the empty tables. As she sat down, she saw with some irritation that Captain Lang was seated at a nearby table. He shifted his chair at an angle so he could look at her while continuing his conversation with Ron Hughes, another pilot. Pretending not to notice him, Robbie stirred sugar into her coffee, while, from under lowered eyelids, she observed him for the first time at close range.

There was no denying his good looks, she admitted reluctantly. His tanned, high-cheekboned face was certainly handsome, with nicely shaped features, and topped by thick, tawny sun-streaked hair. His lean, broad-shouldered frame in the well-fitted dark uniform had an athletic grace.

Suddenly he caught her looking at him, and she saw that his eyes were a clear, gray-blue, full of laughter and an adventurous twinkle. His mouth curved upward in a mischievous smile.

Quickly she opened her handbag and took out Anne's letter. Although she had read it earlier, she needed to divert her attention. As she reread Anne's description of the poverty of the people she served in a jungle mission hospital in Peru and the dedication of the hospital staff, Robbie felt that nagging discontent stirring again. Anne had been one of Robbie's classmates in nursing school and was now utilizing her training to the utmost and making her life count for something worthwhile. It made Robbie feel that somehow what she was doing was rather superficial.

Robbie sighed, refolded the letter, and dropped it back inside her purse. She seemed to spend a good portion of her life sitting around airports, as she was doing today. This winter had been particularly bad—the worst weather anyone in the airlines could remember. Fog blanketed the coast, hanging in heavy pockets that obscured dangerous peaks along the mountain ranges, lowering visibility to zero and causing endless delays, last-minute schedule changes, and cancellation of numerous flights. On the Atlanta-Chicago-Denver and return route that Robbie flew, today's ordeal was a repeat of several such since October.

Why am I doing this? she sometimes wondered. When she had applied for a stewardess job she had imagined a glamorous adventure-filled life of traveling, meeting celebrities, and exciting experiences. What she had not anticipated were long, boring delays like this.

Robbie's thoughts were abruptly interrupted by a teasing voice. "Trans-Con must have selected that color for its stewardesses' uniforms with redheads like you in mind."

Startled, Robbie looked up into T. J. Lang's laughing eyes. She saw that Ron Hughes, with whom she had often flown, had gone for a coffee refill and Captain Lang was leaning across the table to speak directly to her. There was no avoiding an answer of some kind. Unable to feign total interest in the contents of her own coffee cup any longer, Robbie regarded him for a few seconds and then said icily, "The red is a hair-rinse called Amber Glow, and this shade of blue is regulation for Trans-Con stewardesses' uniforms."

Undaunted, T. J. Lang laughed and retorted, "Well, the cute nose isn't regulation; neither is that dimple you're trying so hard to hide. *That* doesn't come with the uniform. And where is all the fabled charm that Trans-Con says their stewardesses have a corner on?" he demanded, grinning.

"Right now I don't happen to be on duty," Robbie snapped pointedly. She wanted to add that "respect for the captain," also emphasized in her training, was not required of an off-duty stewardess either.

Just then, Ron Hughes returned to the table and mistakenly assumed that the two of them were chatting. "Hi, Robbie. Are you flying in this rascal's crew?" he asked.

"No such luck," T. J. interjected. "In fact, we haven't been formally introduced. I didn't quite catch her name."

"This is Robbie Mallory, one of our best stews," Ron said, winking at Robbie.

"Miss Mallory." T. J. stood up and bowed slightly.

"Captain Lang." Robbie acknowledged the introduction coldly.

Captain Hughes, oblivious to the undercurrents, went blandly on. "This young woman is incredible," he remarked. "When she was in my crew, nothing that happened fazed her. I think in one month we had everything on flight from an emergency landing to almost delivering a baby! And Robbie never batted an eyelash! If I could request my flight attendants, I'd have her working every flight I make." He grinned appreciatively at Robbie, who again felt that unwanted color creep into her cheeks under T. J.'s gaze.

She dismissed Captain Hughes's extravagant praise with a shrug and the murmured comment, "All part of the job." In an effort to change the subject, she asked Ron, "Have you seen Jean Ames?"

He shook his head, and eventually the two men went back to their discussion of boats and sailing. Robbie took out the paperback mystery she had picked up at the newsstand and opened it, determined to ignore the disturbing effect of feeling T. J.'s fairly frequent glance.

Less than a half hour later, Robbie's flight was given clearance, and she hurried to the stewardess lounge to freshen up before boarding the plane. There she met Jean, the flight attendant assigned with her to the First Class section for this trip.

"I see you were in the vicinity of old Blue Eyes in the operations lounge. I saw him moving in on you. Should I check to see if you had a sudden increase in heart rate?"

Robbie threw her an amused look and lifted an eyebrow.

"*Me?* I actively resist being attracted to men like T. J. Lang. All that devastating charm leaves me cold."

"I've known more sophisticated girls than you to succumb. He's an expert," Jean commented archly.

"Well, don't hold your breath waiting for me to succumb, Jean. I have no intention of being added to his list. Besides, I'm sure I'm not his type."

Jean raised her eyebrows. "Oh? What type is that?"

"Come on, Jean!" protested Robbie, exasperated.

"As my grandmother and Shakespeare used to say— 'Methinks the lady doth protest too much.'"

Robbie shook her head emphatically. "A man like T. J. Lang doesn't interest me at all." Standing in front of the mirror, she fanned out the tabs on the collar of her aqua silk blouse, straightened her short tailored jacket, and adjusted her cap on her head. Contrary to her flip retort to Captain Lang, her hair actually shimmered with red-gold lights. "I don't know how to convince you!"

"Go on, convince me," Jean urged, as the girls left the lounge and started down the long terminal corridors to their flight's boarding gate.

"Maybe this will surprise you, but my first requirement for anyone I'd be interested in is that he be a Christian."

Jean's eyes widened. "*First?*"

"Yes," Robbie replied.

"It's that important, huh?"

"It is for *me*. Maybe because I've seen firsthand how important it is. Mom is a Christian, but Dad isn't. We have a happy home—my brother and sister and I—but, all the same, we got mixed messages that confused us when we were growing up. Mom took us to church and saw that we attended Sunday school, but Dad played golf or stayed home to mow the lawn or wash the car. Don't misunderstand. He's a wonderful person. It was just that, as I got older, I saw there was something missing in their relationship. He doesn't share the deepest part of my mother's life. So, I don't want to make the same mistake."

Jean frowned. "But weren't there other things that compensated?"

"Oh, sure. Dad makes a good living, and they have some common interests. But when I was old enough to think about lasting relationships, I made up my mind not to get seriously involved with anyone who doesn't share my beliefs. Why waste my time or his in something that won't ever be a complete relationship?"

"Hmmm," Jean said thoughtfully. "I don't know if I could be that positive. I mean, if I had a chance to go out with T. J., even one time, I think I'd go. Just for the experience, you understand!" she giggled.

"I'm not looking for that kind of experience," Robbie laughed.

By this time, they had reached the escalator. Just as they stepped onto the first moving tier, T. J. and his copilot appeared right behind them. Jean gave Robbie a "now what?" look. There was no way to ignore the men and no way to avoid answering T. J.'s question. "Both you young ladies based in Atlanta?"

Although T. J. was looking at her, Robbie let Jean answer. "Yes, but I'm hoping to transfer to Florida to get out of this zero temperature and get some sunshine." Jean gave an imitation shiver.

"I know what you mean. I was based in Miami for the past year and a half, and I miss all the swimming and sailing I did there. But now that I'm back in Atlanta, I'm getting into skiing again. I go up to the mountains in North Carolina every chance I get. Do you ski?" he asked Robbie directly. They had reached the top of the escalator, and he smoothly fell into step beside her.

"I've never tried it," she replied indifferently.

"Never?" He sounded incredulous.

"No, but I've nursed a lot of people with broken bones who have," she retorted shortly.

He smiled. "Well, if I'd known that, I'd have tried breaking an arm or a leg. I bet your bedside manner is sensational!" He grinned wickedly.

She gave her head a little toss and quickened her step, but he kept pace.

They had come to the octagonal lobby with its various departure gates for different flights. Robbie and Jean started one way and T. J. and his copilot had to go in the opposite direction, but T. J. deftly stepped in front of Robbie, towering over her, blocking her way. He whipped a small black address book from the inside pocket of his jacket, snapped open a ballpoint pen, and poised it over the notebook ready to write. "I'd like to call you sometime. Is there a number where I can reach you?"

Amazed, Robbie looked at him. His supreme self-confidence was disconcerting. Caught so off guard, she blurted out without thinking, "I'm in the stewardess roster," and then could have bitten her tongue.

Jean came to her rescue. Tugging Robbie's sleeve, she urged, "Come on, Robbie, we've got to get on board."

T. J. grinned, "Well, I'll be calling you." With a little salute, he spun around and walked briskly toward his own flight gate.

"Do you believe that man!" Robbie demanded as she followed Jean down the ramp and into the plane. *The nerve of that guy!* she fumed silently as she put away her handbag and weekender in the locker. She had only a few minutes to simmer down before the passengers started filing onto the plane. So automatic was her response that none could have guessed that the smiling stewardess welcoming them on board had been seething inwardly moments before.

For the first part of the flight, the two women were very busy, checking boarding passes, helping people find their assigned seats, and assisting with their coats and carry-on bags. After that the stewardesses strolled up and down the aisles making sure all seats were in an upright position and all seat belts were fastened. It was Robbie's turn this trip to give the oxygen mask demonstration. When that was done, she went to her own seat at the back of the section, buckled her safety belt while the plane taxied down the field to its take-off point, and waited for the final clearance from the tower.

As she listened to the familiar sound of the huge jet engines revving and then felt the forward rush and the thrusting lift of the plane, Robbie's mind went back to her first flight as a stewardess and the thrill she had experienced at winning her wings and becoming part of Trans-Con's elite group of attractive, efficient flight attendants. She had brought with her to this job all the qualities that had made her an outstanding nursing student—intelligence, consideration, and a concern for people, blended with a light-hearted, outgoing personality. A sense of fun and a lively curiosity about the world made her ideal for her job. Her nurses' training gave her a competency and calm that was a plus.

The last few years had been exciting and interesting, as well as enjoyable, but sometimes Robbie wondered if she really was fulfilling God's purpose for her life. The question remained in the back of her mind—*Is this enough?*

She could not pursue this line of thought any longer, because the minute the plane was airborne her work began again. She and Jean began assembling the beverage cart for serving. To Robbie's annoyance, Jean took up the subject of T. J. Lang again.

"I think you've really got the high-and-mighty Tyler J. Lang interested. He's sure making a pitch," Jean chuckled.

Robbie frowned. "I hope he didn't get the wrong idea. I certainly did my best to discourage him."

"But that's just it! Don't you see? His ego is involved now," Jean explained as if talking to a toddler. "It's just what he needed to make him determined. He'll have to prove something now." Then she threw Robbie a skeptical look. "Don't tell me you're not the least bit flattered that Trans-Con's gift to women is making a play for you?"

Robbie shrugged, but felt her face grow warm under Jean's scrutiny. There was no more time to continue the conversation as they started down the aisle to serve, but the exchange had disturbed Robbie. After all, to be honest and human, it was impossible not to take *some* satisfaction in an attractive man's attention. Even admitting that much rankled Robbie.

For the rest of the flight, Robbie and Jean worked as a smoothly operating team. They had flown together for the past month, and they moved about their tasks with an even flow. Dinner had to be served next. They set up the trays in the galley, and starting with the passengers seated nearest the galley door and continuing down the aisle, they handled the service quickly and efficiently. All the time they managed to answer all sorts of questions, smile, and attend to various special orders and requests.

Even so, they had just picked up the dinner trays, reshelved them, secured galley cabinets and beverage servers, and gathered up all the containers from passengers lingering over second cups of coffee when the "FASTEN SEAT BELTS" and "NO SMOKING" signs flashed on in the cabin.

The cockpit buzzer sounded, and Robbie lifted the receiver. The copilot gave her the landing time, and she then turned on her hand mike to announce:

We are now making our approach to the greater Atlanta Airport and will be landing in approximately ten minutes. We ask that you adjust your seats to their upright position, extinguish all smoking materials, and fasten your safety belts. It's cloudy and fifty-one degrees in

17

Atlanta. Thank you for flying Trans-Continent Airlines. We hope you enjoyed your flight and will enjoy your visit in Atlanta.

After the plane landed and the last of the passengers had departed, Robbie gathered up her weekender, handbag, and clipboard in order to leave with Jean. The cleanup crew was already on board to make the plane ready for its next flight. The two stewardesses walked through the landing bridge and into the terminal. In the stewardess lounge, they filed their flight logs and checked their mailboxes.

"Here's next month's schedule," Jean remarked as she stifled a yawn. "Wonder who I'll be flying with?"

"Oh, no!" an exclamation of dismay escaped Robbie's lips.

"What's the matter?" Jean asked.

"Wouldn't you know it? I'm on 'reserve' this weekend! That means I'll have to drive right back from Cindy's wedding Saturday to make it."

For Trans-Continent stewardesses, "reserve-standby" meant being available for call to take any flight in case of an emergency or sudden illness of the scheduled stewardesses. Every flight attendant had to take a twenty-four-hour turn each six weeks.

"You can still go to the wedding, can't you?"

"Yes, but I'll have to rush back, probably before the reception is even over," Robbie moaned.

"That's too bad, but maybe you can still catch the bride's bouquet!"

Robbie laughed. What Jean didn't know was that Robbie *had* caught the bride's bouquet at Martie's wedding three years ago—and so far no prospective bridegroom had appeared on her horizon.

Lisa Young, her other apartment-mate, was always telling Robbie that she was too particular—usually when Lisa was trying to persuade Robbie to double-date with her. *"No* man could meet *your* specifications," Lisa had said in exasperation several times.

Was that true or just another of Lisa's exaggerations? Was Robbie cherishing an impossible dream? Weren't there really some men somewhere who wanted the same kind of enduring love that she did?

Chapter Two

The church was filled with afternoon sunshine, throwing dancing rainbows of light through the arched, stained-glass windows. Fan-shaped baskets of crimson-throated gladioli were placed on either side of the altar steps. The deep tones of the pipe organ playing familiar wedding music gradually stilled to a hushed pause.

In the dressing room off the vestibule, Robbie and the other bridesmaids clustered in front of the mirror for a last-minute check of hairdos and velvet halos. When the first resounding notes of Mendelssohn's "Wedding March" were heard, each girl gave a final pat to her ruffled neckline, smoothed down the flounced taffeta skirt, adjusted her bouquet of ruby red roses, and then lined up to start the walk down the long aisle.

Over her shoulder, Robbie cast a lingering glance at Cindy, on her father's arm, and was reassured by her look of radiant happiness. Robbie felt the sudden sting of tears and a peculiar ache in her throat at the expression on her friend's face. As she moved into the measured steps of the processional, Robbie realized the truth of the old saying, "All brides are beautiful." Cindy's pixie-like appearance, transformed by love, had become beautiful.

Taking her place with the other bridesmaids and seeing Mike Gillespie's adoring gaze at Cindy, Robbie could not help but wonder with longing if the kind of love these two shared would ever be hers. Robbie's throat tightened as she watched Cindy lift star-bright eyes to her groom and repeat the solemn promises: "for better or for worse, for richer or for poorer, in sickness and in health, as long as we both shall live." Robbie knew that was what she wanted for herself someday. She would never settle for anything less.

A few hours later, Robbie let herself in the now strangely empty apartment. She had left Lisa still enjoying herself at the reception and, by now, Cindy and Mike were on their honeymoon. With both her roommates gone, Robbie felt somehow abandoned.

Like Cinderella forced to leave the ball, she thought ironically as she set down her suitcase. Because she was on reserve-standby, she had had to leave the reception early and drive back to Atlanta in time to report to the field. It had been hard to leave, with the sound of music and lighthearted laughter in her ears.

Oh, well, there was no potential Prince in sight for me, anyway. Contrary to Jean's prediction, she had not caught the bridal bouquet—not that she believed in any of that silly superstition, she assured herself.

She went around turning on lamps to chase away the gloom of the November evening and to fight the melancholy that had been creeping up on her as she drove home alone. She went back to her bedroom, hating to pass Cindy's bare one, now stripped of all her personal touches, looking bleak and forlorn. Robbie dreaded the thought of interviewing other prospects to move in and help her and Lisa share the rent. Most of all, she knew she was going to miss Cindy dreadfully. They were so close, not only because they had been in the same training class, received their Trans-Continent wings, and lived together for two years, but because they shared a common faith. While in flight attendant school, they had discovered that they were both Christians. That knowledge had created a bond amid all the new surroundings and experiences. Since then their friendship had been a wonderful, strengthening relationship. Their other roommate, Lisa, was easy to get along with and fun, but Cindy had been special.

Maybe I should look for a small place of my own— something I could handle alone, Robbie thought. She had always had roommates, sharing a room with her younger sister at home, then college and nursing school with Martie, and now this apartment with Cindy and Lisa. She did not look forward to the hassle of getting used to a new roommate and adjusting to someone else's idiosyncrasies. With Cindy married and Lisa possibly transferring to Texas to be closer to her boyfriend at SMU, it might be a good time to think about a change.

However, the prospect of watching the newspaper for apartment ads and making the rounds to check them out seemed unappealing—even downright depressing! *What is the matter with me?* Robbie wondered crossly. Maybe there was nothing like a wedding to make one feel lonely.

She snapped open her suitcase and pulled out her bridesmaid's dress, holding it up and surveying it severely. What would she do with a used bridesmaid's dress, especially one which four other girls she knew had duplicates of? If she risked wearing it to a party, all four might show up wearing the exact copy! Even remodeling it seemed futile. *So what then? Ditch it? Donate it to a thrift shop? Decisions, decisions!* Robbie sighed.

What she needed right at the moment was a nice, hot shower.

Under the warm needle spray, she shampooed her hair and felt some of the tension and fatigue ease. She resolved to fix herself something to eat, then go to bed early and get a good night's sleep. Stepping out of the shower, she toweled off and wrapped herself in her cuddly, if worn, chenille robe that was softly comforting. She wrapped her wet hair turban-style and headed for the kitchen.

Suddenly the phone began ringing and she ran barefoot to grab the receiver. "Hello!"

"Field Operations calling," the clipped voice at the other end identified himself. "Roblynn Mallory?"

"Speaking," she said breathlessly, reaching for a notepad.

"You're scheduled out tomorrow, Flight 224. 0900. Okay?"

"Okay. Destination?"

The voice chuckled. "Lucky you. Better pack a bathing suit. It's *Bermuda!*"

Robbie hung up the phone and drew a long breath. All her depression vanished. *Bermuda!* A run she had always thought would be glorious—but so had several hundred other stewardesses far above her in seniority. She had never dreamed she would get the assignment on a reserve call. She knew the crews had a three-day layover there, and visions of coral beaches, cloudless skies, warm ocean breezes, and blue surf came floating into her mind.

She went at once to her closet to look for appropriate clothes to take with her. All of her summer things were zipped into plastic bags in the back of the closet, and it took her some time to pack for this unexpected holiday.

For a "holiday" it seemed after all the trips through Chicago's winters and Denver's snowcapped mountain weather, and even Atlanta's chill. By the time she had settled on a simple, wrinkle-proof wardrobe to see her through any possibility that the trip could present, Robbie realized she was famished and went to the kitchen to begin the search for food which her phone call from Operations had postponed.

The contents of the cabinets were not too encouraging—and exploring the refrigerator was even less appetizing. Peering into it, Robbie saw some diet colas, two cartons of fruit yogurt, some bananas that had seen better days, a dozen eggs, and a jar of pickles. There was also a fading corsage and a couple of packages of Lisa's pantyhose, which, for some reason, she believed lasted longer if they were frozen before wearing. Since Lisa had been the only one of them home last week and was on a continual diet to keep her required weight, Robbie was not too surprised by the empty larder.

Settling for scrambled eggs, Robbie got out a small frying pan and stuck two pieces of whole wheat bread in the toaster. Breaking eggs into a bowl and whisking them briskly, she recalled with amusement Cindy's culinary experiments. After she had become engaged, she had enrolled in cooking classes, and Lisa and Robbie had been treated, or *subjected*, as the case may be, to many elaborate menus. Some of them had been disasters, but others had turned out great.

Affectionately, Robbie remembered how conscientiously Cindy had prepared for her new role of wife. She had brought home books from Christian bookstores on the subject of marriage and its responsibilities as well as its joys. And Mike Gillespie was just as serious as Cindy was about the new life they were starting together; both had taken premarital counseling at their church.

As she washed the dishes after her solitary supper, Robbie thought of the minister's words at the close of the ceremony today: "If true love and an unselfish spirit guide your relationship, you can expect the greatest measure of worldly happiness. The rest is in God's hands, nor will He be wanting when you humbly submit those needs to Him."

Was it possible to achieve those ideals in today's world? Most of the people Robbie encountered seemed to have a rather cynical attitude toward marriage. The airline's gossip mill sizzled with tales of philandering married pilots and transitory relationships. It seemed to accept and give tacit approval to the rumored swinging single life lived by stewardesses and other flying personnel. Of course, not *all* airline employees felt or lived that way. Still, it was considered the exception, not the rule, to be faithful and to have certain standards, and those who did were looked upon as fanatics or nuts! Robbie sighed. Even Jean had questioned her ideas.

"Well, I don't care! I know what I want and it's worth waiting for!" Robbie announced emphatically out loud, then laughed. "Better watch it, girl, when you start talking to yourself!" She wrote a note to Lisa explaining about being called out on flight and stuck it on the refrigerator door. "At least, you don't get any arguments when you do!" Yawning, she turned out the kitchen light and went to her bedroom.

The buzzer of her alarm clock awoke Robbie from dreams that were a mixture of the wedding, flight procedures, and scenes of turquoise waves swirling in lacy curves onto pink sand beaches. An hour and a half later, looking fresh and clear-eyed, Robbie was in

Trans-Continent Operations, signing in on the crew sheet for her flight.

"Well, good morning," a voice behind her said. It had a tantalizing familiarity about it, and Robbie turned around slowly to see Tyler Lang ambling toward her.

"You!" she gasped.

"Just checking out my crew," he told her.

"Your crew? Flight 224?"

"The very same," he replied lightly.

"Oh, no!" she exclaimed, then clapped her hand over her mouth.

Tyler threw back his head and roared with laughter. "Surprised, eh?" he demanded teasingly.

Robbie suppressed a nervous giggle. "Well, of course, I mean, yes. I didn't think to ask about the pilot on this flight. You see, I was on reserve and—"

"You might have tried to get out of taking this flight if you'd known who the captain was?" he persisted.

His amused eyes met hers and, in spite of herself, Robbie laughed. "No. I'm just . . . well, it does seem rather a coincidence . . ." her voice trailed off.

"Fate, maybe," Tyler said, raising an eyebrow.

Robbie was saved from further embarrassment by the arrival of another stewardess, Stacy Culver, who greeted them both and added her name to the crew sign-up sheet.

"Well, it looks like this crew is going to pretty-up the Bermuda landscape enormously," commented T. J., including Stacy in his glance. Just then the copilot, Clive Amory, and the flight engineer walked in, and the three men went to check the weather readings and file their final flight plan.

Robbie let out her breath slowly. *T. J. Lang again. What kind of strange coincidence is this!*

Chapter Three

"This flight is really fun," Stacy commented as she and Robbie took their places at the plane's entrance, ready to check boarding passes of oncoming passengers. "We call it the 'Honeymoon Express.' Bermuda must be the honeymoon capital of the world. We get a lot of newlyweds and people celebrating anniversaries. Some tell us they spent their honeymoon there and want to go back for their twenty-fifth or even their fortieth anniversary." She rolled her eyes and said dryly, "Of course, we don't get many of *those* these days! But anyway, there's always a happy atmosphere on these flights."

Robbie discovered that Stacy was right, as couple after couple boarded. Some were obviously honeymooners, the girl wearing a corsage, her young husband beaming. Other twosomes were more discreet. But there was plenty of handholding and starry-eyed looks being exchanged even before takeoff.

"What did I tell you?" whispered Stacy. "Two by two just like into the ark."

As Stacy predicted, the flight, although busy, was very satisfying. First of all, there was the elegant, special brunch of mushroom omelets, crisp bacon, pecan rolls, and fresh fruit, served with sparkling cider or dark, fragrant coffee. Robbie and Stacy took off their jackets and caps and donned attractive cover-all aprons in Trans-Continent's colors of azure blue and turquoise. The cabin hummed with the buzz of conversation, laughter, and good-natured banter among the passengers.

While most of them were enjoying a second cup of coffee, Robbie ducked into the galley to pour herself a cup of the reviving beverage and take a break.

"Any of that left?"

Robbie looked up and saw T. J.'s broad-shouldered figure filling up the narrow entry to the galley.

"Plenty," she replied and reached for a coffee mug and handed it to him.

Stacy had carried the breakfast trays to the cockpit earlier, so this was the first time that Robbie had seen T. J. since their unexpected meeting in Operations that morning.

There was something about T. J. Lang that both annoyed and attracted Robbie, and she found this very confusing and uncomfortable. She did not like feeling confused about people. Tyler Lang had a most peculiar and puzzling effect upon her.

"Your first trip to Bermuda?" he asked as he poured his coffee.

Robbie nodded.

"You'll love it. Everyone does."

"So I've heard."

"Great place for lovers," he remarked. His eyes on her were sparkling, his smile enigmatic. He jerked his head toward the First Class section. "They're all so preoccupied with each other, you and Stacy should have a fairly easy job this trip." When she made no comment, he inquired, "Got any plans for after we land?" After another pause, "If not, I'd really like—"

28

Whatever he was going to say, Robbie never got to hear it because, just then, Stacy stepped into the galley, her arms full of new magazines. "Would you believe that no one, but no one, is interested in reading the latest issue of *Time* or *Newsweek*?"

They all laughed. Then Tyler asked Stacy, "What are your plans for the layover?"

"Shop, what else? I've got a Christmas list a yard long. I can't wait to get into all those fantastic shops. Wait 'til you see the cashmere sweaters, Robbie; you'll go crazy. And the prices!"

"I guess that answers my question." Tyler chuckled and put down his coffee mug. "Well, ladies, I'd better get back and fly this plane. I don't want to keep all those Hamilton shopkeepers waiting."

After he left, Stacy sighed deeply. "What a dream, right? I wonder who the current lucky lady is? Sometimes I'm tempted . . . I mean even *if* . . . as they say, his interest in anyone only lasts about three weeks, it might be worth it!" Stacy laughed. "No! Scratch that. On second thought my Pete's more in my league. That is, if he ever gets through graduate school!"

At that moment, a stylishly dressed matron with exquisitely coiffed hair and wearing a Cardin suit looked into the galley.

"Excuse me, but would you happen to have a deck of cards on board?"

"Sure, just a minute." Stacy smiled accommodatingly and went to find the cards.

Left alone for the moment, Robbie tried to guess what Tyler Lang had been about to suggest when Stacy had interrupted. *Offer to take me around Bermuda? Hardly! Why would someone like Tyler consider playing tour guide to someone like me! We could not be more different.*

The adage, "opposites attract," thrust itself into Robbie's mind, and she brushed it away impatiently. *Forget any irrational possibilities,* she chided herself. *Tyler Lang and I live in two different worlds.*

When she got to Bermuda she would spend her time shopping, swimming, sunning, and just relaxing, and return to Atlanta with a good tan. And that was that.

There was the usual excited stirring among the passengers as the plane began its descent. Buckled into her own seat by this time, Robbie pressed her face against the small window, eager for her first glimpse of Bermuda. Could it really be the island paradise the travel brochures claimed and even Trans-Continent's own "Bermuda Holiday," as the folder advertised?

As the plane banked, Robbie saw a stretch of crescent beach with sand as delicate a pink as the inside of a shell, and water the dazzling, unbelievable shades of blue, turquoise, and jade. As they flew in lower, she saw green hillsides dotted with rainbows of flowers and houses in pink, blue, yellow, and pale green—looking for all the world like a toy village.

Once the plane landed and the door was opened, Robbie stood at the entrance bidding good-bye to the deplaning passengers. Breathing the soft, balmy air, she knew that Bermuda was going to live up to all her expectations.

She wanted to go exploring immediately or even to give in to the temptation offered by the hotel's sparkling swimming pool which she and Stacy passed on their way to their cottages, but Stacy could not wait to take Robbie shopping and let her see for herself all the marvelous specialty stores. Assuring herself that there would be plenty of time for everything in the next three days, Robbie changed out of her uniform into cotton slacks and shirt and joined Stacy to go into Hamilton, the capital of Bermuda.

At first Robbie was overwhelmed as she followed Stacy from store to store and saw the abundance of items to be had—the lovely woolens, beautiful porcelain, silver and English china, coral jewelry and fine leathers, all at more reasonable prices than they could be purchased in the United States. This, along with the tasteful displays and the courteous clerks, all in an unhurried atmosphere, added to the pleasure of shopping.

No one seemed annoyed if Robbie was not ready to buy but simply wanted to browse. Instead of being a frustrating or tiring experience, even with a tireless shopper like Stacy, Robbie enjoyed every minute of the spree. The ambiance of Bermuda itself wove its spell of quiet charm from the soothing pastel colors of the buildings and the presence of abundant flowers everywhere. After the hectic pace of city stores and the sameness of suburban shopping malls, Robbie found it all a welcome change.

When at last Stacy had come to the halfway mark on her Christmas list, and both girls had their arms loaded with various packages, they came back to the hotel.

On the path back to their adjoining cottages, they met Tyler Lang, dressed for tennis in white shorts and a short-sleeved knit shirt, contrasting sharply with his deep tan. In the sunlight his hair gleamed like burnished gold. He stopped and asked with a smile, "Well, did you two buy out the shops?"

"Not quite," Stacy admitted, "but there's always tomorrow."

"How about my buying the weary shoppers a drink?" T. J. suggested.

"Sounds great." Stacy agreed without a consulting glance at Robbie.

Without appearing bluntly rude, Robbie hardly could refuse. Reluctantly, she went with them to a table on the terrace. There was always a special camaraderie among the crews when on layovers, and Robbie had flown long enough to know that, unless you wanted it otherwise, things *stayed* simply friendly and casual. On most long layovers, and when a crew had been flying together for a period of time, everyone went his or her separate way. Once in a while a special relationship happened, but it was up to the individuals what they wanted to do off duty. There were no set rules of conduct. But, since this was her first time with this particular crew on this flight, she felt somewhat obligated to let Stacy take the lead.

Under ordinary circumstances, Robbie would have had no objection. She knew that it was Tyler Lang's unsettling effect on her that she minded. She would have liked to keep their relationship confined to "on flight" and strictly professional, but this casual encounter would not change that.

They were seated at a table beside the pool under a bright blue umbrella when the waiter came for their order.

T. J. asked, "Well, ladies, what's your pleasure?"

"I'll have iced tea," Robbie said.

"What? Aren't you going to sample Bermuda's special welcome drink, a rum swizzle?" Tyler asked in amazement.

"No thanks. Iced tea sounds good to me," Robbie replied evenly.

"But it's traditional!" he persisted. "Especially for a first-time visitor."

"Iced tea is what I want," Robbie maintained, beginning to feel annoyed that he was making such a big deal of it.

"You're sure? The no-alcohol ban for crew members only applies to twenty-four hours before flight time."

Robbie turned and looked directly at him. "Yes, I know."

Tyler shrugged slightly, but she saw a hint of reluctant admiration in his expression before he turned his head to give the order to the waiter.

Robbie stirred uncomfortably. What difference should it make to T. J. Lang that she did not drink? Unless it made *him* uncomfortable. Robbie had never felt it necessary before to explain herself, and she was determined not to be embarrassed by doing so now.

The other two ordered rum swizzles. Their copilot, Clive Amory, sauntered up and joined them just then. While he and Stacy discussed presents Clive might take home to his wife and children, T. J. turned to Robbie and asked, "So, what was your first impression of Bermuda?"

"Well, about all I've really seen so far is the inside of some fabulous shops."

"There's a lot more to see than a few streets and the interiors of gift shops and boutiques. I'd suggest—"

T. J. was interrupted by Clive's asking, "Ready to get beaten to a pulp, fellow?"

"I'm ready to take you six-love the whole set!" T. J. retorted. Amid the laughter, the talk then turned to tennis. After they finished their drinks, the men excused themselves and left for the tennis courts.

On the way to their cottages Stacy told Robbie about a quaint little restaurant nearby that served a typical

Bermuda menu and suggested they go there for an early dinner. Robbie consented.

She was surprised to discover that the meal had a decidedly Southern flavor. Hoppin' John, a dish of rice and black-eyed peas, was labeled "an original Bermuda recipe" and served with ground beef cooked with tomatoes and green pawpaws. A rich dessert with layers of guava jelly and thick cream followed.

Tired from the flight and their shopping excursion, the girls parted for the night, each to her own cottage. Robbie indulged in a luxurious bath and fell asleep to the sound of reggae music wafting through her open window from the hotel terrace. She dreamed happily of the two whole days still to be spent in Bermuda.

Chapter Four

Robbie woke up to a room filled with sunlight. A soft breeze billowed the sheer curtains on the floor-length windows. She raised herself on her elbows and looked out through the translucence of the draperies to cloudless blue skies and a deeper blue ocean that stretched endlessly to the horizon.

Her first morning in Bermuda! It seemed like a fairy tale to awaken to all this sun-drenched beauty. Robbie surveyed the pleasant bedroom, with its bamboo furniture and polished chintz pillows in subtle patterns of blue and lemon. A basket of fruit and a bouquet of fresh flowers rested on the dresser.

Robbie had been surprised to discover that Trans-Continent crews on layovers were given the same kind of individual pink stucco cottages as other guests of this luxurious hotel. Nestled under palm trees along the many winding paths that spread over the manicured grounds, each little unit was secluded in flowering borders of hibiscus and oleanders.

So this is how the proverbial "other half" lives, Robbie thought, stretching lazily in the pillowed comfort of the queen-size bed.

There were so many enticing possibilities for the day ahead that Robbie was not sure what she would do first.

Finally, in spite of the luxury of lying in bed, she flung off the covers and bounded up. Happily Robbie sang the words of one of her favorite Psalms set to music: "This is the day which the Lord hath made! We will rejoice and be glad in it!" She found her bathing suit, put it on, and headed for the swimming pool.

It was still early, and the pool area was empty. Quickly Robbie shed her terry-cloth robe and slipped out of her clogs. She went to the deep end and dived in. The sharp, plunging coolness of the water rushed around her as she surfaced and then struck out with firm strokes across the pool. The water sparkled in the morning sunlight, and the air on her face was fresh. A singular kind of gladness coursed through her body as she swam. What fun to have the whole pool to herself, to twist and float, dive and dip in its sun-dappled depths! She might as well be a millionairess in her private pool and have this whole beautiful, flower-bordered area as her personal estate. Robbie delighted herself fantasizing as she swam back and forth several times.

At length, she got out, dried herself lightly, and stretched out on one of the cushioned lounge chairs. She put on dark glasses and shut her eyes, feeling the warm morning sun needle into her bare skin. She was utterly relaxed after her invigorating swim.

Robbie was not sure how long she had been sunning when the sounds of the diving board's spring and the splash of water caused her to open her eyes and sit up slightly. She was just in time to see Tyler pull himself out of the pool.

His tanned, muscular body glistened with water in the bright sunlight. He tossed back his wet hair and climbed the ladder to the high diving board again. Positioning himself carefully, he leaped up for a spring and then jackknifed into the pool—an expert dive, Robbie noted. When he came out of the pool once more, he looked her way, lifted one hand in a wave, and then started toward her.

No wonder females from fourteen to forty are captivated by his looks, Robbie mused with reluctant appreciation, watching him. His long-legged, lean, but powerfully built body clad in brief black trunks moved with easy athletic grace along the edge of the pool to where she lay.

"You're getting an early start on the day," he greeted her. "More shopping? Does Stacy have you booked for another raid on Hamilton shops?"

She shook her head.

"Good. Then you can let me show you some other aspects of Bermuda. There are so many choices. There's St. George—a day in itself. It takes you back to colonial times. Or a glass-bottomed boat cruise to see the undersea wonders, or the Crystal Caves, or the Botanical Gardens. What do you say?"

For a fraction of a second, Robbie hesitated. All sorts of warning signals flashed in her brain. She remembered all the stories she had heard about T. J. Lang's fatal charm, all the sad tales of other stewardesses permanently hurt by brief flings and sudden finales. Was his reputation as a heartbreaker warranted? There was one way to find out, of course. What could be the harm of a casual, daytime sightseeing date with this attractive, interesting man? Besides, he knew Bermuda, and she did not relish being dragged through the shops again today with Stacy. So, why not?

"Are you sure you want to do the 'touristy' stuff?" she asked cautiously. "After all, you've seen all those places. Won't you be bored?"

"Bored? I'm never bored. I don't tolerate boredom."
He smiled, his square teeth dazzling white against his
tan. "Anyway, I believe only boring people get bored.
Come on, let's go! I'll meet you in twenty minutes in
front of the hotel."

A half-hour later Robbie found Tyler, wearing a dark
blue sportshirt and khaki pants, waiting for her where
the winding path leading from her cottage crossed the
hotel's boat landing. "We'll take the ferry across the harbor, and then the island bus over to St. George. It's a nice
ride, and you'll get to see more of everything," he told
her.

Once seated in the front of the boat and moving across
the rippling blue water, Robbie felt the wind tossing her
hair and blowing refreshingly on her face. She was glad
she'd said yes. Spontaneously she looked up and smiled
at Tyler, sitting beside her in the rapidly moving craft.

With the sun sending coppery sparkles through her
hair, Captain T. J. Lang noted that Stewardess Roblynn
Mallory was even more attractive out of uniform. He
liked the yellow poplin skirt, the yellow and green
striped blouse, and the bright green espadrilles. She had
style, he concluded, congratulating himself on his taste.
He smiled broadly back at Robbie. Yes, indeed, the day
ahead held promising possibilities.

When they got off the bus in St. George, Robbie felt
as if she had stepped backward into another century.
The colonial atmosphere was so far removed from today
that the whole place might have gone to sleep three hundred years before.

They walked along the enchanting, small, winding
streets, seemingly untouched by the passing centuries.
There were flowers everywhere—in window boxes, in
clay pots, and spilling over the low stone walls in front

of the houses. The busy streets and bustle of Hamilton had been left far behind, and Robbie was caught up in a magical time warp.

Crossing King's Square, Tyler pointed out the stocks and pillory used in the seventeenth century to punish offenders. "You know Bermuda was discovered almost by accident. English colonists on their way to Virginia were caught in a storm at sea and shipwrecked."

"An 'ill wind that blows no good,' right?" Robbie quipped.

"Right!" T. J. gave her an amazed look. "You're a Shakespeare buff? Then, maybe you know he used Bermuda as his prototype for the island in *The Tempest*?"

"No! I have to admit I didn't know that!" laughed Robbie.

Tyler halted and raised his eyebrows. "Am I being pompous? Showing off?" he asked.

Robbie shook her head, still laughing. "No, not at all. I'm fascinated. Really!"

"You're being honest?" He looked doubtful.

The expression on his face surprised her. It even looked a little sheepish. It seemed oddly out of keeping with her first impression of him as an arrogant person. He looked genuinely worried that he might seem conceited.

She raised her hand in a mock salute and said, "Scout's honor!"

They looked at each other and laughed.

After that little incident, the rest of the day took on an entirely new aura. Her original wariness of him gradually melted, and they developed a delightful camaraderie. T. J. was an interesting and informed companion, sharing all sorts of little insights about different places and things not found in tourist brochures.

The next two hours passed quickly as Robbie and T. J. wandered around this perfect gem of a town brimming with unexpected treasures. Almost every building had an historical significance of its own.

They visited St. Peter's, a charming little church and the oldest Anglican place of worship in the Western Hemisphere; and the "Old Rectory," now a library. Both places had their stories, and T. J. told them with relish as if he enjoyed sharing something that he himself found fascinating. He took Robbie to the house which, during the American Civil War, was the home of a Confederate agent. It was there that many conspiracies had been hatched and many plans for blockade running plotted by the rebellious adventurers of that day.

The time went by so pleasantly that Robbie was surprised when Tyler announced that it was well after noon and asked if she were hungry. She realized she was.

He took her to a lovely small restaurant where their lunch was served in a garden patio under flowering trees that gave shelter from the hot sun. They enjoyed delicious seafood salad, chilled melon, tiny individual loaves of banana-coconut bread, and coffee.

When their waiter refilled their cups for the second time, Robbie sighed with contentment and looked around her with pleasure. "This has really been delightful. Thank you," she said.

"It's been my pleasure, actually," Tyler replied. "It's great fun being with someone who so obviously enjoys everything. So many people play at being sophisticated, thinking it's uncool to express any real enthusiasm or enjoyment. But you're different—so open, transparent. It's a very nice change."

Change from what, change from whom? Robbie could not help wondering. Is that what he found interesting about her? That she was "different"? Robbie was not sure she knew exactly what he meant or whether she liked being called "different."

He crossed his arms and leaned forward on the table. He looked at Robbie quizzically, saying, "Tell me about yourself. I know by now that you're more than a pretty face." He smiled warmly. "And I know you're more than a smiling representative of Trans-Continent Airlines. I'm curious about what's underneath that poised surface—what you do on your time off, what kind of books you like, what kind of music you listen to—lots of things. In fact, everything!"

"Everything?" she exclaimed. "That's a tall order. Isn't it more fun to find out about a person little by little?"

"Maybe, if you have lots of time. But you and I live on airline time, and both of us know what that is. Our paths have never crossed before and chances are that—" he paused. "Given our flying schedules, who knows when we'll get an opportunity like this to get to know each other?" he explained. "Maybe I'm just curious. Indulge me. You see, I can't understand why we've never met before now. How long have you been with Trans-Con?"

"Nearly three years," Robbie answered.

"See? I've been with the airline five, and we've never been assigned to the same crew before this flight! I'm trying to make up for lost time. Now, begin," he directed.

"There isn't all that much to tell. I grew up, went to high school in a small town in Ohio, and went away to college with my best friend as my roommate. We both decided to go into nurses' training, and the next year we enrolled in the Good Shepherd Hospital program. Then,

41

in my senior year, a Trans-Con stewardess came to talk to our class, and I applied for training."

"In search of travel, adventure—and *romance*?" T. J. prompted.

"Well, adventure and travel anyway," she laughed.

"No romance? Isn't there someone special in your life?"

"No, no one. Not at the moment." She felt like squirming under his skeptical glance.

"That's hard to believe."

Flustered, Robbie reached for her purse and sweater. "Believe it. It's true. Shall we go?" She wanted to end this line of personal questioning.

T. J. rose, held out her chair for her, and said, "I'm sorry if I embarrassed you, but your diplomacy is a fine example of Trans-Con's training. You know how to deal with pushy inquisitive males."

Robbie looked up at him and said archly, "See that you put that in your flight report, Captain."

"For sure!" He put his hand under her elbow and smiled down at her as he guided her deftly through the tables and out again into the street and the afternoon sunshine.

They strolled leisurely along the curving narrow streets, pausing here and there to admire a window display of fine china or ruby glass or antiques. Then they turned into a side street, no more than a small lane, and came quite unexpectedly upon a bay-window gift shop and art gallery tucked between two other stores.

Entering the gallery, they found it to be well lighted with nicely hung paintings of flowers, seascapes, and some familiar Bermuda landmarks. As they wandered about, Robbie spotted a small, watercolor painting that immediately caught her eye. She moved nearer and stopped to have a closer look.

It was of a pink, white-shuttered, typical Bermudian cottage, nestled in a cluster of flowering, wind-twisted trees. In the foreground was an irregular cobblestone wall, over which clambered climbing roses. A small wooden gate stood open, as if inviting one in to the charming garden.

Tyler came and stood behind her while she gazed. Finally she said softly, "I think I'll buy this if it's not too expensive. It really captures Bermuda for me, and who knows when I'll get back here? I always like to have something special from a place I've been to take home with me—to remember it by."

He was watching her with a thoughtful expression. "Wait here. I'll go ask the gallery manager the price." He was gone and Robbie continued to look at several other paintings by the same artist. Then she returned to stand in front of the one she still liked the best.

Tyler came back and told her how much the small painting was.

"Wonderful!" Robbie said excitedly. It just happened to be well within the price range she had mentally allowed herself to spend.

The purchase made and the painting wrapped and tied, they walked back to King's Square and boarded the bus to the ferry landing. Seated beside her, Tyler seemed preoccupied looking out the window. After a while he turned to Robbie, tapped the painting, and asked, "Is that a picture of your 'dream house'?"

"Oh, I don't know. But it is something one might dream of owning some day," she said somewhat shyly.

"I think it is, maybe subconsciously. You impress me as the kind of girl who would dream of living in a rose-covered cottage with all that implies."

"Is that bad?" she asked, feeling a little uncomfortable under his penetrating gaze.

"Not bad, just different. Most women nowadays think more along the lines of a luxury high-rise condo complete with swimming pool, Jacuzzi, and sauna," he laughed, shrugging.

"Well, of course, this particular cottage would have to be set on a cliff overlooking a coral beach in Bermuda!" Robbie smiled.

They arrived at the ferry landing just in time to board the ferry back to the hotel. It was beautiful crossing the bay in the late afternoon. The water was a mosaic of deep blue-green and golden reflections from the low-slanting rays of the sun. They sat quietly, enclosed by the sights and sounds of being on the water, but Robbie did not feel uncomfortable at their lack of conversation.

It was only when they got back to the hotel that she felt slightly awkward. She did not want him to feel trapped into spending the evening with her, so she held out her hand and said, "Well, thank you for a wonderful day, Captain Lang."

There was a glint of irritation in his eyes. "*Captain Lang?*" he repeated.

Robbie felt her face redden and she said quickly, "Tyler—or do you prefer T. J.?"

"Most of my friends call me Ty," he said brusquely.

"Well . . . Ty . . . thanks for everything."

For a moment, she thought he was going to say something. Then he just nodded and spun around, heading toward the hotel with long strides.

She stood there looking after him, watching his tall figure enter the hotel bar. For some reason the pleasant afternoon dimmed. Something subtle had changed the nice flow between them. Robbie was not sure what, but she had definitely felt a coolness.

Well, whatever had changed the atmosphere between them, she was not going to let it spoil the memory of her experience in St. George. It had been wonderful, and she had this marvelous little painting to help her remember a beautiful day.

Suddenly feeling tired, Robbie decided to take a swim. The idea of relaxing in the pool, then showering and going to bed sounded wonderful.

Most of the swimmers had departed for the hotel lounge or an evening at some of the many tourist attractions the island offered. Again Robbie had the luxury of the pool almost to herself. After a refreshing, relaxing hour she returned to her cottage, on the way passing several couples holding hands or with their arms about each other's waists, strolling toward the hotel terrace. For a moment Robbie felt a pang of indescribable loneliness, a sudden longing to belong to someone who loved her with all the singleness of passion, caring, and tenderness of these honeymooners. She recalled her answer to Tyler Lang's probing this afternoon, when she had said there was "no one special" in her life just now. It was true, and she felt a sudden sadness about it. Would it ever be different for her? She was still troubled by a lingering melancholy as she opened the door of her cottage.

To her surprise, her phone was ringing as she stepped inside the bungalow. She was even more surprised to hear Tyler's voice, asking, "How would you like to go on a picnic tomorrow?"

"A picnic?" Robbie echoed, startled.

"I was just sitting here thinking about you, and it struck me that you were the sort of girl to take on a picnic. I know this marvelous little cove, a kind of private beach, an easy distance from the hotel where we could spend the day swimming and looking for shells. So what do you say?"

"It sounds like great fun," she said, conscious of an excited little tingle.

"Can you ride a moped?" was the next question.

"As a matter of fact, yes!" she answered. The last time she had gone home on vacation her younger brother had just bought one, and Robbie had learned to ride one then.

"Fine! The hotel will fix us a box lunch to take along. I'll meet you in front of the hotel about nine."

Feeling foolishly happy, Robbie hung up.

Chapter Five

With a cloudless blue sky overhead, the sun warm on their backs, and the cool wind of early morning on their faces, Robbie and Tyler maneuvered the rented mopeds along the winding road leading from the hotel to the beach.

Wheeling along under the crimson canopy of arched poinciana trees, they passed through typical Bermuda residential sections. The pastel colors of these uniquely painted homes, mingled with the glorious multicolored flower gardens, reminded Robbie of French impressionist paintings.

They waved to groups of children in bright uniforms walking along the roadside on their way to school. The youngsters smiled and waved back.

"Almost makes me feel like we're playing hooky!" Tyler called to her after they had sped by a cluster of uniformed schoolboys.

"I know! Me, too!" laughed Robbie.

In a way, that was exactly how she did feel. All this beauty surrounding her, the sense of expectancy about the day ahead, and the feeling of freedom, combined with another, not so easily defined sensation, gave Robbie a lightheadedness. She had never felt so buoyant or so full of a kind of incandescent joy. She glanced over at Tyler, and he was smiling, too.

"We're almost there!" he shouted. "Make a slow right at the next turn."

They veered off onto a side road that was nothing more than a footpath, and she slowed her moped to follow his in single file.

"We can park our bikes here and climb down to the cove," Tyler said, rolling his moped over behind some hibiscus bushes. He then turned and took hers. He removed the basket containing the box lunches the hotel had packed for them, and held out his hand to Robbie. "Come on, I can't wait for you to see my favorite beach."

The path was hidden from the roadway by the full, flowering bushes on the hillside, but it was an easy descent for Robbie, following Tyler.

When they reached the bottom and Robbie saw the crescent of pink sand and the curve of turquoise water rolling onto it in lacy scallops, she gave a small gasp of pleasure. "Oh, how perfect!"

"I knew you'd love it!" Tyler grinned. He set down the lunch basket, along with a daypack he'd carried, and then challenged her, "Let's not waste a minute. I'll race you into the surf."

They had worn their bathing suits under their clothes. It took Robbie only a moment to unzip her jumpsuit and run down to the ocean's edge. T. J. was right beside her and grabbed her hand as they plunged into the waves. For at least a half hour they dived, ducked, swam, and bodysurfed like two playful dolphins. Then they floated leisurely on the swells for another half hour.

Every once in a while, Robbie felt like pinching herself to be sure that she actually was enjoying herself a world away from her everyday life. It was pure fantasy to be sure!

Finally, breathless and panting, they waded into shallower water and onto the beach. They stood at the water's edge breathing deeply and laughing.

"That was some dip!" Tyler shook his hair out of his eyes. "And you're some swimmer. I was beginning to wonder if you had fins!" His eyes swept over her slim figure in the striking blue maillot.

Robbie suddenly felt self-conscious, as much aware of herself as of Tyler, whose sleek, muscular body was glistening in his swimsuit like molten bronze. To cover her inner confusion she exclaimed, "I'm absolutely starved. Let's see what's in our box lunches." She started walking toward the spot where they had left their things.

Tyler threw her a speculative glance but only said, "Sure, let's go."

"So this is what Bermudians call a picnic!" commented Robbie as they opened up their boxes. "It looks more like a gourmet feast!"

Tyler took the small tablecloth that had been folded on top of the box and spread it out between their two beach towels. With a sly grin he handed her a folded cloth napkin. "You've heard of Englishmen dressing for dinner in the jungle, haven't you? Well, Bermudians picnic in style."

"You can say that again!" Robbie murmured as Tyler began to unpack plastic containers. Immediately he repeated, "Bermudians picnic in style."

Robbie laughed. She couldn't remember when she had laughed as much as she had today with Tyler.

Hungry from the fresh air, sun, and exercise, they ate heartily of the delicious food—sliced breast of chicken and crusty French rolls accompanied by small containers of butter, mayonnaise, mustard, olives, and pickles. There was also paté, rye crackers, fresh pears, lemon pound cake, and two thermos containers—one of limeade, the other of hot coffee.

As they sipped their coffee, Robbie watched the breakers roll in cobalt curves and spread in lazy arcs on the sand. She sighed contentedly and, when she turned to say something to Tyler, found him staring at her.

He smiled and squinted his eyes and asked, "Do you believe in fate?"

"I don't know. Possibly," she replied slowly.

"Did you ever wonder how I happened to be taking this flight and you were called in on reserve to work it?"

She shook her head. "Not really. I was surprised, but . . ."

"I've been flying vacation-relief," Tyler told her. "That's how I happened to be in Chicago the day we met. Doesn't it strike you as strange that those two unrelated incidents brought us together?"

Robbie's heart quickened unaccountably. Where was Tyler's train of conversation leading them? *Into dangerous territory* was her second thought. "I'm afraid I don't have the answer to that. I take things pretty much as they come," she said lightly. Then she changed the subject quickly by asking, "How did you start flying?"

"I got into it in college, did my service stint in the Navy, and got into commercial flying after that."

He seemed to take her cue, and their subsequent conversation became light and general. In a little while it trailed off entirely, and they stretched out on their towels to sun.

Robbie gazed at the seemingly endless horizon. The water flowed onto the pink sand in variegated shades of blue, from azure to sparkling sapphire to jade. Above, seagulls swooped with lavender-tinged wings against the cloudless sky. It was all so beautiful that it made her heart soar with unexpected happiness.

Watching the roll of the breakers had a mesmerizing effect, and Robbie began to feel drowsy. At the same time, she was very aware of Tyler lying beside her, only an arm's length away. It was a situation tingling with provocative possibilities—the two of them on a deserted beach, alone, thousands of miles from anyone who knew them. Robbie thought of all the things she had heard about Tyler. Had it all been hearsay? Rumor? Fabrication? She did not know what to believe. Tyler's behavior toward her had been above reproach. There had been nothing to make her feel uncomfortable or apprehensive, even in a situation that might be considered potentially intimate. He had been a perfect Southern gentleman.

The more she was with him, the less Tyler resembled her preconceived ideas about him. Maybe he had projected a certain kind of image to make himself less vulnerable, accessible. Or, maybe, as she had originally stated to Jean, she was definitely not his type. But what *was* his type? What sort of girl would T. J. Lang really fall in love with? Who would induce him to make a forever kind of commitment?

Robbie sat up suddenly, hugging her knees. Beside her, Tyler raised his head and asked, "Something wrong?"

"No. I was just thinking that this is nearly as perfect a day as I can imagine," she declared, looking out at the sea. She took a handful of sand and let it sift through her fingers. "I just wish I could somehow take it all back with me and on those gray days pull it out and live it all over again."

"You could bid on this run," T. J. suggested.

"Me and a hundred other stews with more seniority!" she laughed.

This has been a wonderful day, maybe the best of my life so far, Robbie thought with startling clarity. She turned to look down at Tyler's tawny head resting on his folded arms, his lean, tanned body stretched out alongside her, and she drew in her breath. Had it been because of him? She would certainly never have had days like yesterday and today if it had not been for Tyler Lang. The fact that he had chosen to be with her, making her time in Bermuda so special, created a funny little quiver. Was it possible, after all her determination to resist, that she was falling under the magnetic spell of this worldly, sophisticated pilot?

Just then Tyler stirred, stretched, and languidly pulled himself to a sitting position. He glanced at her with a reluctant smile. "I hate to say it, but I guess we'd better start back."

"I know," she agreed, sighing.

Overhead drifting clouds threw abstract patterns on the sand in purple shadows. Whitecaps whipped by a brisk wind danced on the blue-green sea.

The wind off the ocean was growing chilly as they gathered up their belongings and started up the hill to where they had left the mopeds. Robbie was ahead on the path up the slight incline, with Tyler following, when a stone rolled under her foot and she suddenly slipped backward, almost losing her balance. His arms caught her and held her until she steadied herself—and then a little longer. Feeling the strength of his arms around her, Robbie was newly aware of him, but she lingered only a moment. Then, laughing somewhat self-consciously, she told him, "I'm okay now." She pulled away and ran the rest of the way up.

But whatever had happened in those few seconds, Robbie felt shaken by it and a little frightened. Was it possible that she was just as susceptible to Tyler's legendary charm as all those girls she had pitied for falling for him?

"I hate to see this day end," Tyler admitted after they had turned in their mopeds and were walking along the flower-bordered paths behind the hotel to their cottages. He caught Robbie's hand, swinging it slightly, then halted at one of the little recessed vistas overlooking the harbor. "Let's sit here and watch the afterglow."

He gestured to the white, wrought-iron bench facing the ocean. They sat down together, gazing out at the shifting colors painted by the evening shadows on the now-quiet sea. A flash of rainbow sail caught Robbie's eye, and she watched as a small boat drifted into its mooring for the night. Gradually, like filmy silk scarves flung carelessly, streaks of pink, mauve, violet, and orange spread across the sky.

Tyler's arm draped along the back of the bench casually found Robbie's shoulder. His hand touched her hair and gently turned her head toward him.

This close, Robbie saw that his eyes were more blue than gray as she had thought. Neither were they cold or calculating, as had been her first impression. As he looked at her now, they seemed kind and almost tender.

"Have dinner with me, Robbie. This is our last night in Bermuda and I don't want to waste it. Clive and the others were talking about going out to some bistro and listening to a band that's all the rage now on the island. But I'd rather not. What I'd like is a quiet dinner for two— *just us*—on the hotel dining terrace. How about it?"

"What about the others?" The last thing that Robbie wanted was false rumors circulating about her and Tyler.

"On these layovers I've found that people do pretty much what they want to—live and let live. Besides, I really don't care. Do you?"

Suddenly Robbie knew she didn't. All she knew was that she wanted to spend this last evening in Bermuda with Tyler—alone.

Robbie was just getting out of her shower when there was a rap on her bungalow door. "It's Stacy!" a voice called out. "May I come in?"

Robbie slipped into a short terry-cloth robe and shouted, "Sure!"

Stacy Culver opened the door and plopped down on the nearest chair. "For once I am shopped out!" she declared. "But I got through my list! And everybody better be happy with their presents because I'm almost dead!" She paused and then eyed Robbie speculatively. "You sure pulled a disappearing act. I stopped by before I went to breakfast to see if you wanted to go with me today and poof! No Robbie. I came home later and you *still* weren't here. You missed tea," she said accusingly. "And when I say you *missed tea in Bermuda,* you really missed something special. It's the real thing. Lovely brisk tea with lemon or real cream, tiny little cucumber and tomato sandwiches, a fantastic cake, filled with fruit and nuts—" She broke off abruptly and demanded, "Where in the world *were* you anyway?"

Robbie could not suppress a happy little smile as she told Stacy about the beach picnic with Tyler.

"Uh-oh!" Stacy's arched eyebrows and sly smile spoke volumes.

"It's not what you think!" protested Robbie quickly.

"No?" Stacy was all wide-eyed naivete. "Tell me about it!"

Robbie gave as casual an account as she could manage of her day at the cove with Tyler.

"Why don't we discuss it more in detail over dinner? Want to go to that same little restaurant?" Stacy asked.

There was a long moment of awkward silence. Then Stacy got to her feet, holding up both hands as if to ward off some flimsy excuse. "Nope, don't bother to explain. I just hope you know what you're doing, Robbie." She started toward the door. "Good luck!" she called over her shoulder and was gone.

Robbie stood for a minute looking after her. There was no denying Stacy's unspoken implication. *She doesn't understand,* Robbie told herself as she began to towel dry her russet-brown hair. *We enjoy each other's company, that's all. Why not spend the evening with someone you find interesting and amusing, and who finds you attractive?* Robbie gave her head a defiant little toss. *I'm not going to make more of this than there is.*

But as she dressed and hurried to meet Tyler, she felt as if little wings had sprouted on her feet. *How many other girls have felt the same way about him?* she asked herself anxiously. But she refused to answer her own question.

Chapter Six

Robbie saw Tyler before he saw her. He was standing at the top of the terrace steps looking out at the harbor, his handsome profile etched against the dark blue evening sky. She felt extravagantly happy as she ran lightly up the steps and he turned to meet her, his eyes lighting up with pleasure at the sight of her.

His approving glance swept over her, making her feel confident and pretty. She wore a sleeveless dress that was the color of ripe peaches; it was especially becoming with the glow the day in the sun had given to her skin. Her high-heeled sandals showed off her delicate ankles and shapely legs and made her look taller.

"Bermuda certainly agrees with you," Tyler told her. "You look positively blooming."

Robbie had bought the dress on impulse at the end of last summer in an expensive boutique, paying more for it, even on sale, than she would ordinarily spend. But now she felt that her indulgence had been worth it.

"You look mighty sharp yourself," she told him. He did, in a natural hopsacking blazer, gray slacks, and blue oxford cloth shirt. "We both look like we actually belong here! Bermuda is a way of life I could easily become accustomed to."

"I knew you would," Tyler said assuredly, guiding her to their reserved table overlooking the ocean.

Dinner was a harmonious medley of gourmet food, good conversation, and guitar music provided by a small trio of brightly costumed native musicians. The atmosphere was so delightfully unreal that Robbie felt as if she were living in some kind of dream.

Time passed so swiftly and pleasantly that Robbie was startled to notice most of the nearby tables were empty, and couples had moved to the larger terrace where dancing had begun.

T. J. reached over and took one of her hands. "I'd suggest we join them, but we both know we have a six o'clock wake-up call and have to be out at the field at seven."

Robbie sighed. "Yes, I know. It's all gone so quickly. Tomorrow we may be back in rain and sleet and all this will be just a—"

"Dream?" he prompted.

"A memory." She smiled. "An unforgettable one."

He looked at her for a long time before speaking, then said, "Don't be so pessimistic. You may be back in Bermuda again sooner than you think."

"I wish I thought so." She smiled wistfully.

"Haven't you heard of the power of positive thinking?" he teased as he rose from his place and came around and held out her chair for her. "I'm a great believer in going after whatever you decide you want in life."

"And do you always get it?" Robbie asked curiously.

"Most of the time. And when I don't, it's usually because I didn't want it badly enough in the first place."

They went down the shallow terrace steps and across the grass to the paths that led back to the cottages. The air was fragrant with the scent of frangipani; the breeze softly rustled the fronds of the palm trees lining the way. Over all the moon shed a silvery sheen. They walked in silence, the only sounds their footsteps on the crushed shell path and the rhythmic reggae melodies floating from the dance pavilion.

As they neared her cottage, he slowed and reached for her hand. The feel of his palm against hers and the strong grip of his fingers as they closed over her hand sent little tingles rippling through her and made it suddenly difficult to breathe.

The small lantern outside her cottage door was lighted and, as they walked up to the doorstep, its light silhouetted Tyler's profile. He halted on the steps and took both her hands. Raising them to his mouth, he kissed her fingertips and said, "I've been to Bermuda a dozen times at least, but this has been a very special time. It's *you*, Robbie, who made it so special. Do you have any idea how tempting you are, Robbie?"

Then he was holding her, his chin resting on the top of her head. He brushed back her russet hair with one hand, tucking it behind her ear. Then she felt his lips on her temple, the side of her cheek, the edge of her ear. She heard him whisper her name. He turned her head slightly, and his kiss covered her mouth. For several moments she was caught up in his strength and tenderness.

"Robbie, you're so sweet, so very special—and beautiful. But, luckily, you don't know it. That's what makes you so—" he broke off. In the pale light filtering through the overhanging trees, Robbie saw him smile and frown a little, too, as if at a loss. "Good night, and thank you. Sweet dreams, little lady."

For some reason Robbie felt a small ripple of alarm. T. J. sounded as if he were saying more than good night. It sounded more like *good-bye.*

"But I'll see you in the morning," she said.

"Sure, in the morning. Seven sharp." He touched her cheek softly and turned away, walking with long, swift strides. Soon he had disappeared into the shadows.

Dazed, Robbie went into her cottage, closed the door behind her, and leaned on it for a moment, taking a long, deep breath. She felt lightheaded, happy, yet sad; exuberant, but a little depressed; bewildered and still incredibly alert.

Had that embrace really happened? Or had she simply dreamed it? She could still feel the pressure of his hands on her shoulders; the warmth of his kiss on her lips; and the disturbing effect he had on her.

Was it only the moonlight, the music, the magic of Bermuda? Or had she made the mistake of falling in love with a man who probably would break her heart?

By the next morning, Robbie began to feel as if it *had* been a dream or even a figment of her imagination. In the van on the way to the airport, Tyler was remote and impersonal. He did not come back to the galley once during the flight back to the States, and by the time they landed in Atlanta, Robbie was convinced that Tyler J. Lang was proving true to form. *A fling, that's all it had been—two and a half days to amuse himself in Bermuda with a new conquest.*

Robbie tried to cover her inner hurt by smiling more and filling up the time on flight chatting lightly with the passengers. But her throat ached with the effort at small talk, and her face felt stretched from the strain of smiling. She was hoping desperately that she could hide her humiliating embarrassment until she got home.

What a fool she had been to think that he had meant anything of what he had said or the flattering attention he had lavished on her for that brief time!

She had just seen the last passenger off the plane and down the ramp, and turned to get her handbag and weekender out of the locker when Tyler emerged from the cabin. *No escape,* she thought with a sinking heart.

"Could I drive you home?" he asked.

She was stunned. He was smiling, easy and relaxed. *What kind of game is he playing?*

"No thanks, I've got my car," she stammered.

He tipped his hat and gave her a little salute and said, "Well, then, I'll call you later." And he was gone, walking with long strides along the ramp and into the terminal.

Robbie stared after him in disbelief. Happiness flooded all through her again. She tried to tell herself she was crazy. She shouldn't allow any man to put her on this kind of emotional seesaw. But even as she scolded herself for being so relieved that he had promised to call, she felt scared.

Deep down inside, Roblynn Mallory had the silly premonition that, somehow, Tyler Lang was going to change her life irrevocably.

Chapter Seven

"I'll call you later," Tyler had said.

But two days later, he still had not called.

It was almost time for Robbie to leave on her next scheduled flight; so even if he did call, she would be out of town.

Two hours before she was to leave for her Chicago-Denver trip, Robbie stood in her apartment kitchen and glared at the phone.

Maybe the whole thing, the "Bermuda experience," as she began facetiously to call it, had added up to a big zero—a three-day interlude in her life—enjoyable, fun, exciting, romantic. But, she was not at all sure she would ever hear from T. J. again. It had been just happenstance that they had been scheduled on that flight together. Their paths had never crossed before and might never again.

Part of her mind told her that, but another part was not so sure. Every time the phone had rung, she had felt a surge of hope, followed by disappointment and self-doubt. His evident indifference should have confirmed her first impression of Tyler Lang. But somehow, it didn't.

Robbie thought she had caught a glimpse of another side of Tyler Lang that no one else had ever seen. He had charm, tact, and distinction, but they were the surface of his personality. What lay beyond was what interested Robbie. Was there character there, some foundation of beliefs, or only a determination to wall the real inner person from prying eyes, keeping him immune to emotional involvement, protecting him from love? Under that easy exterior, what kind of man was really underneath?

Robbie thought of her conversation with Stacy Culver on the first leg of the flight back to Atlanta from Bermuda. While they had been stashing trays in the galley, Stacy had cast several speculative glances at Robbie and then said hesitantly, "I don't mean to pry—well, yes, I do! I have to confess I'm bursting with curiosity. What have you been up to the last two and a half days?"

Robbie had turned to her, wide-eyed and with simulated bewilderment. "Whatever do you mean, Stacy?"

"Come on, give!" Stacy had demanded, her eyes brightening eagerly. "I mean, besides his being the eighth wonder of the world, how did you happen to spend so much time with our illustrious captain?"

"Are you asking what do I see in him?" Robbie had asked, again feigning puzzlement.

"Robbie!" exclaimed Stacy in frustration.

Robbie laughed easily. "There's nothing to tell really! Nothing to start the Trans-Con grapevine buzzing. We just had a great time together. Sightseeing, mostly! And if you're asking 'what is Tyler Lang really like?', all I can say is that he's intelligent, charming, witty . . . what else?" Her eyes sparkled mischievously.

"Oh, you're too much!" Stacy lifted her shoulders hopelessly. "I don't know any other stew he's spent practically a whole layover with, and you act like it's no big deal."

Robbie had just smiled and finished fastening the tray lockers. She had not wanted to fuel the gossip mill with too many details of the last couple of days. She did not know Stacy well enough to trust her not to spread a lot of false rumors.

Robbie opened her refrigerator door and took out the ice tray and banged it irritably against the edge of the sink to dislodge a few cubes. She pulled the metal tab off the can of diet cola and poured its contents into a glass. Staring out the window over the sink, she sipped her drink, thinking. *He won't call. He's never going to call. Ever!* she concluded. *Well, so what?* She had other things to think about, other things to do besides wait for a silly phone call.

She had been invited to spend Thanksgiving with her nursing school roommate, Martie Evans, and her husband, Tom. Robbie was looking forward to that. Lisa Young's transfer had been approved, and she would be leaving at the end of the week. That left Robbie with the problem of finding new roommates or looking for a smaller place of her own.

When she left for the airport, she took the day's newspaper along, determined to examine the apartment rental ads and to start checking some out. What she needed was a new environment, a fresh outlook, a different view.

Forget him, she commanded herself. *If he hasn't called by now, he isn't going to call.*

But he *did* call.

Returning home from her flight, Robbie automatically checked the recording device on the phone and found three messages from Tyler Lang! Listening to his warm, exciting voice with its hint of a drawl, she felt an unexpected thrill.

She turned off the answering machine and sat down in wonder. It had happened after all. She felt her heart do funny little somersaults.

Do I return his call? Robbie asked herself. Maybe the question really was *should* she return it.

No matter how attractive Tyler was and how intriguing the idea of going out with him might be, Robbie felt uncertain. Tyler had a reputation for "loving and leaving." Wasn't she playing with fire? Was it worth the risk that she too might be caught in a dangerous flame?

Robbie decided to wait for a while before calling him back. On her layover in Denver she had spotted an interesting ad in the Atlanta paper for an apartment back in Atlanta. She had called from the airport before coming home and made an appointment to see it that afternoon. That would give her time to think about what she wanted to do about Tyler.

SPACIOUS GARAGE APARTMENT, the ad read. NEWLY REMODELED, DECK, LR, BDRM, BTH, MODERN ALL-ELECTRIC KITCHEN, PRIVATE ENTRANCE, ONE CAR SPACE AVAILABLE.

The address led Robbie to a two-story frame house in a residential area. It was neat and freshly painted with a large porch and well-kept lawn, located on a pleasant, tree-shaded street in an older part of town.

Robbie parked her small car in front and took a critical look. There was a driveway that curved around to the back, and Robbie could see the building behind the house that must be the garage over which the apartment was built. It had a balcony something like a Swiss chalet and an outside staircase. If the inside of the apartment was as inviting as the exterior, it seemed promising. Robbie got out of the car, walked up to the porch of the house, and rang the front doorbell.

A gray-haired, sweet-faced lady of about sixty answered. She was Martha Holmes, the owner. As she took Robbie to show her the place, she explained that the apartment had been built for her son and daughter-in-law to live in while he attended Georgia Tech.

"But now they've moved to Texas, and it's been empty for nearly a year. I never really planned on renting it—"

As Mrs. Holmes was showing her the apartment, a persistent meowing caused Robbie to look down at her feet and see a big, fluffy marmalade cat with a beautiful white ruff and eyes gleaming like peridots.

"Oh, that's Cyrano," Mrs. Holmes explained. "Don't let him make a nuisance of himself. Jeff and Donna couldn't take him with them when they moved. Even though he's my cat, he spent a lot of time up here with them and must still think of this as a part-time home."

"Oh, I wouldn't mind. I love cats. We aren't allowed to have any pets in the building I'm living in now."

Afterwards, Robbie thought it was Cyrano who had really cinched the deal and settled her indecision about taking the apartment.

After a long, rambling conversation in which Robbie expressed her love of antiques and her interest in having a garden, Mrs. Holmes brought out a lease, and they went inside to sign it over a cup of tea.

It was late by the time Robbie got back to her own apartment. To her surprise and delight, she found another message from Tyler waiting! This time he had added the information that he had tickets to the ballet, *Sleeping Beauty*, next week, and he wondered if she would like to go.

Sleeping Beauty! She adored ballet, and of course she would love to go. All the cautious reservations she had had about seeing Tyler Lang again vanished in her excitement. Her heart did pirouettes as her fingers whirled the digits of his phone number on the dial.

After his "hello," Robbie had barely identified herself before he said with a low chuckle, "Well, finally! I was beginning to wonder if I'd dreamed you up or if you were some kind of myth. I'm glad to know you're real."

They chatted for a few minutes, and then he began to explain why he had not called her soon after they had returned from Bermuda. His excuse was plausible enough. "My next assignment after the Bermuda hop was a long flight to the West Coast. While I was there, a buddy talked me into taking a few days' leave and flying to Hawaii. When I got back here I started dialing your number—with no luck until today."

It was all very understandable and, because Robbie wanted to, she believed it. When he asked her about going with him to the ballet, Robbie tried to keep her voice calm and casual. "What's the date? I'll have to check my flying schedule."

"A week from Thursday."

"Hang on a minute and let me check."

She already knew that, in case of a conflict, she would find a way to switch flights with another stew in order to be free that evening.

Back on the phone, she said, "That will work out fine. I'd love to go."

"We'll have dinner first," Tyler said smoothly. "Since the performance begins at eight-thirty, I'll pick you up a little after six, so we'll have plenty of time for a leisurely dinner."

"That sounds fine. I'll see you a week from Thursday."

The moment the phone clicked, ending their conversation, Robbie had second thoughts. Hadn't she decided that Tyler Lang was not the best person for her to date? What had happened to all her resolutions about forgetting him?

But the ballet, she argued. She couldn't miss a chance to see this company do *Sleeping Beauty.* What girl in her right mind would turn down an invitation like this?

But she wasn't acting like a girl in her right mind, Robbie admitted sheepishly to herself in the days before their date. Even though she had kept telling herself it was just a date, she had done some wildly crazy things, such as splurging on a new outfit and an outrageously expensive little beaded bag to carry. She had even considered having her hair done but settled for a manicure instead. Hairdressers had done some weird things to her naturally wavy hair in the past, she recalled in time.

The new dress she bought was a sophisticated royal blue sheath with a matching quilted velvet jacket. And she found sleek four-inch-high heels.

She shuddered mentally as she cut off the price tags and tossed them in the wastebasket without a second look. *That's what comes of letting your heart rule your head.*

But when she had finished dressing on the evening of the ballet, she knew that the outfit was perfect. Her mirror assured her first, and later Tyler's low whistle confirmed her impression.

"You look smashing," he said as they left the apartment building. His shining black sports car was at the curb, and he opened the door for her to get into its red leather bucket seat.

"I thought we'd go to the Midnight Sun," he said as he slid behind the wheel and started the engine. "It's close to the High Museum where the ballet's being performed. That way we won't feel rushed through dinner."

"Wonderful!" murmured Robbie. She had never been to the Midnight Sun but had heard it was one of the plushest dining places in Atlanta.

The maitre d' nodded to them and said, "Good evening, Captain," as they entered the restaurant. Tyler confirmed his reservations, and they were led through the quiet, carpeted room of early diners to a curved banquette in the corner. Robbie was not unaware of several heads turning as they passed, conscious of a few envious glances from women seated at tables they passed. Tyler, she noted, after she was seated and had a chance to look around, was undeniably the best-looking man in the room.

He was also, she discovered, completely at ease in the elegant surroundings. He commanded respect as he gave their order after consulting with her for her preference. When he asked for the wine list and she shook her head, he said smoothly, "A tonic and lime for the lady, a glass of Chenin blanc for me," and handed it back to the waiter without comment about her not joining him.

Over dinner Robbie again was impressed at Tyler's wide range of interests as they discussed topic after topic, from politics to plays. Robbie had spent a lot of time with pilots and noted that so many of them had limited conversational abilities beyond aeronautical matters.

Dinner itself was worth discussion—coquilles St. Jacques, fresh vegetable mélange of broccoli flowerets and baby carrots, rice pilaf, and salad. They had just enough time for coffee before leaving for the theater.

Robbie had been to the High Museum before, but she never failed to thrill at the magnificence of its interior with deep crimson carpet and beige-gold marbleized walls. She enjoyed seeing all the well-dressed people streaming up the two staircases into the auditorium. Her anticipation of the ballet made her especially animated. Her eyes sparkled and her face was glowing as they went up the steps and were ushered to their seats.

Although Robbie kept her eyes on the printed program, it was impossible not to feel T. J.'s nearness. Her breath became constricted as if she were holding it. She almost wondered if he could hear her heart's sudden pounding. Mercifully, the houselights darkened and the music began. Silently T. J. reached over and took her hand.

The performance of Tchaikovsky's great masterpiece was transporting. The scenery, costumes, music, and, most of all, the perfection of the dancers completely enthralled Robbie. When the bows of the principal dancers had been taken, a bouquet of roses was presented to the prima ballerina. She withdrew one rose from it and gave it to her partner, and the applause became deafening.

The houselights came up, and people began to leave. Programs were dropped, and the noise of conversation rose to a high level as people moved up the aisles, commenting excitedly on the performance.

Robbie felt dazed. The 1889 ballet had been so beautiful that it was hard to come back to reality and the present moment.

"You really enjoyed it, didn't you?" Tyler asked as they came out into the night. "I watched you during the performance, and you were totally taken up with the stage and everything that was going on. It's really refreshing to see someone so openly enjoying something!"

As they got in his car, he asked, "Would you like to go somewhere for a drink or coffee or—" he smiled indulgently, "a hot chocolate?"

She had to laugh. "No thanks. I'd better call it a night." She had managed to be in town for tonight's date, but she did have an early flight out the next morning.

At her apartment door she thanked him. He held out his hand for her key and unlocked the door for her.

"I'll call you," he told her.

"Will you?" she asked, her eyes shining in the dim light of the foyer. His words had a familiar ring.

"Yes," he said and leaned toward her.

"Oh, I almost forgot," Robbie exclaimed. "I'm moving. Here's my new address and phone number, just in case." She opened her small purse and handed him a slip of paper.

He touched her cheek softly. "I'll call you," he promised and left.

Chapter Eight

The next few days were hectic. Robbie barely had time to move to her new apartment before her next scheduled flight, so she could leave to spend Thanksgiving with Martie and Tom Evans. She had not visited her friends yet in the house they had just bought, and she was anxious to see it. And she was eager to see how their baby girl, Tessa, had grown.

Although the Evanses lived only sixty miles from Atlanta—a little over an hour's drive—Robbie and Martie's lives had taken separate paths since Martie's marriage three years ago. They talked often by phone and always remembered each other's birthdays and special occasions with cards and notes. If Robbie's flight schedule allowed it, they tried to get together whenever Martie and Tom came to Atlanta to shop or see their families.

But zipping along the freeway on Thanksgiving morning, Robbie realized how much she had missed her friend and looked forward to one of their old-time talks. She particularly wanted to confide her feelings about Tyler Lang to Martie.

Driving through the quiet suburb, following the instructions Tom had given her, Robbie pulled up in front of a gray-shingled Dutch colonial house with blue-shuttered dormer windows and a neat lawn enclosed in a picket fence. *Right out of a storybook*, Robbie smiled suddenly, recalling something that Tyler had said to her in Bermuda.

You impress me as the kind of girl who would dream of living in a rose-covered cottage with all that implies.

He was right, thought Robbie. *The house is exactly suited to Martie—and me!* Both of them were small-town girls with the same romantic ideals. The only difference was that Martie's dream had come true.

Robbie got out of the car and approached the house. She pushed open the gate and, as she did, the front door opened and a slim girl with pale blonde hair came dashing down the steps to hug her.

"Oh, Robbie, I'm so glad you could come!" Martie exclaimed happily.

Tom appeared in the doorway holding a curly-headed, rosy-cheeked cherub in his arms. Smiling broadly he called out, "Welcome to the Evans estate!"

"Some neighbors are coming for dinner, too," Martie told Robbie as she showed her into the small slant-ceilinged guest room, "and a bachelor friend of Tom's from work."

Robbie looked up from the suitcase she had just opened and regarded her friend suspiciously. "You wouldn't!" she accused. "Are you and Tom match-making again?"

Martie looked innocent. "Of course not!" she said indignantly. "Would I do something that obvious?"

"I don't know," Robbie said doubtfully. "I remember how we used to sit in the dorm late at night and plan how we'd marry men who worked in the same office and have houses next door to each other."

Martie wrinkled her nose winsomely. "That still sounds wonderful to me!" she declared. "But, no, seriously, Alan's just a nice guy. I don't think you'd be very interested, actually. Is there anyone currently in your life?"

In spite of trying to act nonchalant, Robbie felt her face get warm. "Well," she began, "maybe. It's something I want to talk to you about later."

There was no time then because Thanksgiving dinner was planned for four o'clock and the guests would be arriving a little earlier. Other people were bringing things to add to the meal, but Martie was cooking the turkey. The Evans kitchen was warm with the tantalizing odors of roasting turkey, onions, and herbs.

"What can I do?" Robbie asked.

"How about mashing the potatoes?" Martie suggested, getting out the electric mixer and taking the large pan of boiled spuds off the stove.

"I can't wait to hear about your new interest!" Martie said, smiling, her face flushed from the heat of the oven as she withdrew a casserole of yams. "I hope it's someone who deserves you." She placed tiny marshmallows on top of the steaming mound of mellow orange fluff and sprinkled them with chopped pecans before returning the dish to the oven.

"Would *anyone* deserve me in your opinion, Martie?" Robbie laughed.

"Well, you thought Tom was perfect for me," she countered.

"And he was—*is*! You're a perfect couple!"

"Lucky is more like it."

"It's more than that," Robbie said seriously.

"Yes, you're right. But we couldn't do it alone. You know that, Robbie. Our faith in God is the center of our lives, and that's what makes the difference."

Tom pushed open the swinging door from the dining room and announced, "Maxine and Ted are here!"

Soon after the arrival of that couple, Alan Downing, the "bachelor friend" from Tom's office showed up. He was a quiet but articulate young man, and Robbie liked him, but anyone she met now seemed a pale contrast to T. J.

The next half hour or so was busy with chatter, laughter, and good fellowship. Robbie liked those who had been invited to share Thanksgiving and felt right at home in the friendly atmosphere. As they all gathered around the dinner table with little Tessa's high chair alongside her daddy's chair, there were compliments on the colorful setting. The table was beautifully arranged, festive with Martie's best china, dazzling crystal, and gleaming silver—all shining in the glow of four tall tapers. In the center a milk-glass compote held a luscious assortment of fruit resembling a Cezanne still life.

Martie beamed with pleasure and appreciation before turning to her husband. "Tom, will you ask our blessing?"

"We hold hands," Tom said quietly to everyone, and each person clasped the hand of the one standing next to him. He prayed,

Heavenly Father,
Thou who clothes the lilies
And feeds the birds of the sky,
Who leads the lambs to pasture
And the deer to the waterside,
Who hast multiplied loaves and fishes

And converted water into wine,
Do Thou come to our table
As Guest and Giver to dine.
Amen.

The feast was eaten amid much laughter and merriment, with good-natured kidding among the men about the football game they had watched earlier on TV. There were some groans and protests when Martie offered a choice of apple or pumpkin pies, but everyone, it seemed, had room for a *small* sliver. It was the kind of holiday that, although she enjoyed it thoroughly, made Robbie conscious of the longing tug in her heart for just such a home and family of her own.

After the other guests had left, Robbie helped Martie bathe Tessa and tuck her into her crib in her snuggly pink sleeper. When they returned downstairs, Tom had put the dishes in the dishwasher and made a fresh pot of coffee. Grinning, he stifled a yawn and told them, "I'm going to bed and read for a while and let you girls catch up on all your news."

"What a nice guy," Robbie remarked as Tom went upstairs and she and Martie settled into opposite ends of the living room sofa with their coffee.

"I couldn't agree more!" giggled Martie. "Now, tell me all about you and this new man."

Robbie began her account of Tyler by telling Martie the funny way she had met him and all the coincidental things that had seemed to bring them together. As she talked about him, she was more aware than ever how much he had occupied her thoughts lately.

"I don't know what it is, Martie. In one way, I don't think he's right for me. But on the other hand, I've never felt quite this way about anyone else. I mean, when I'm around him I feel . . . different."

"How different?" Martie pursued.

"Well, excited! Happy! Hot, cold, trembly—" Robbie broke off, laughing self-consciously. "Confused! Dizzy!"

"It sounds more like some kind of virus!" Martie said, and they both dissolved into silly laughter.

"If I thought I could have what you and Tom have, . . ." Robbie said thoughtfully, "but I don't think Tyler is even a Christian."

Martie looked at her friend a long time before replying. "I know you, Robbie, and I don't think you'd do anything impulsive, but do go slow, won't you? Don't let your feelings run away with your good sense. Stick to what you know in your heart that you really want out of a marriage. It's for the rest of your life, you know, and you don't want to make a terrible mistake."

They talked for quite a while longer. At last overcome by weariness, they both trailed off to bed. Robbie had to leave the next morning, since she was scheduled out on a flight the following evening. She and Martie had a little more time for sharing confidences the next morning after Tom left for work and before Robbie had to start for Atlanta.

"It's been wonderful having you here. I wish you could come down more often," Martie said wistfully. "That way I could meet this pilot you've landed and keep tabs on you!" She smiled. "You're my best friend, and I wouldn't want to see you get hurt."

Robbie frowned. "I hope I haven't given you the wrong impression of Tyler."

"Just that he's a Greek god!" Martie teased. "And every woman's dream."

"Well, not quite," Robbie said, then added, "but almost!"

Martie walked out to the car with Robbie and gave her friend a hug. "Take care, won't you, Robbie? And write or phone; let me know how things are going."

"I will. And don't worry about me. My head may be in the clouds, but my feet are on the ground," she assured Martie.

"But your eyes are filled with dreams," Martie said softly.

Driving back to Atlanta on that crisp winter day, Robbie thought affectionately of Martie. She was glad she had had a chance to confide in her about T. J. Robbie could always depend on Martie to listen sympathetically and give sound advice if it was asked for. But had there been a note of caution in Martie's response to her enthusiastic accounts about her developing romantic relationship?

Of course, T. J. Lang was not the "ideal husband" Robbie had outlined so specifically when she and Martie had been roommates. Maybe that was why Martie was reserving full approval.

Robbie remembered a greeting card Martie had sent her once with such a lovely sentiment on it that Robbie had saved it. "A faithful friend is a strong shelter; and he that hath found one, hath found a treasure."

Robbie had certainly found that in Martie. Would she find that same quality in Tyler?

Chapter Nine

On Saturday morning in the second week in December, Tyler phoned Robbie at her new home above Mrs. Holmes' garage.

"How are you at Christmas shopping?" Tyler asked. "I need some help with mine."

"You called the right number," Robbie quipped. "I worked as a personal shopper in a department store in my hometown during the Christmas rush when I was in high school."

"You know, I have a talent for picking the right person for the right job. Maybe I should be in personnel work instead of flying," Tyler laughed. "I'll buy you lunch if you can solve the problems on my list, okay?"

"It's a deal," Robbie replied.

"I'll pick you up in an hour," Tyler said before he hung up.

They went to Phipps Plaza, a complex of fine shops and branch stores of some of the best nationally known retailers. With Tyler's list in hand, Robbie seemed to have an uncanny knack for thinking of the right gift and the good luck to find most of the items she thought of. With Tyler providing the cash or credit card for each purchase, shopping was easy and fun.

Two hours later, they sat at a table in The Peasant Uptown, a charming restaurant delightfully decorated in green and white, with latticed chairs and hanging plants. Pots of red and white poinsettias were massed at the entrance and along one wall. The eatery was a refreshing oasis from the hustle and bustle of the shopping center.

"You're incredible," Tyler told Robbie, shaking his head. "I'd still be wandering around in that mall like a rat in a maze. I can't believe we got everything accomplished in such a short time."

Robbie affected a brisk, professional manner and replied, "Our service thrives on satisfied customers such as yourself, sir. I just hope you'll give others your recommendation."

Tyler smiled but continued, "Seriously, you could go into business doing this sort of thing! I know a dozen men who would be willing to pay good money for relief from this chore. Taking you to lunch, however, I consider *my* bonus!" He leaned across the table and said, "How come you're so smart and so pretty, too?"

Robbie's face colored, making her lovelier than ever. She was grateful that their order arrived at that moment. She took a bite of her sandwich and said, "This is delicious repayment. Hardly seems fair to get treated for doing something I enjoy. Besides, I love spending other people's money!"

Tyler took out a rumpled piece of paper and a ballpoint pen and started checking off items. "Let's see— the candlesticks for Aunt Louise, the cosmetic bag for my cousin Jan, deerskin slippers for Uncle Jim, sweater for Ellen, my niece—what did we get for my sister and her husband? Oh, right! The 'Toby' coffee mugs." Tyler finished checking off the list with a flourish. After pocketing his pen he grinned broadly. "I feel like a great weight has been lifted off my shoulders. Now what shall we do with the rest of the afternoon?"

Impulsively Robbie suggested, "What about iceskating?"

Tyler's eyes lit up. "Great idea! Come on, let's go."

They drove across the city to the indoor skating rink and were soon skimming the glazed surface with the ease of skaters who had often skated together. Holding hands, cross-armed, they circled the frozen arena several times, enjoying the feel of their runners cutting into the ice.

"Hey, you didn't tell me you were another Dorothy Hamill," Tyler said after a few spins around the rink.

"It's one of my well-kept secrets," she retorted.

"I'm discovering new things about you all the time," Tyler said with a kind of puzzled edge to his voice.

"That's what makes life interesting, don't you think? You believe you know all there is to know about someone, and then suddenly you find a whole new facet of his personality that you hadn't even suspected."

"I think that's what you tried to tell me in Bermuda, wasn't it? That first time we went out together I wanted to find out all about you at once. You thought I was moving ahead too fast, didn't you?"

"Maybe," Robbie replied noncommittally. She was not yet ready to tell Tyler all the reservations she had about getting involved with him.

"I think you were right. Too much too soon can ruin a relationship. It's probably better to build a foundation for friendship that can lead to—" he stopped and suddenly whirled her into a spin, very carefully, expertly, and they began skating backward, doing a few intricate steps.

80

Afterwards Robbie thought maybe that had been a clever maneuver on Tyler's part—a tactic to avoid letting down his guard. She was sure she knew the logical ending to what he was saying—a foundation for friendship that can lead to *falling in love*.

Even with all he obviously thought and felt about her, Tyler was not ready to speak of love. Nor was Robbie ready to make a similar declaration.

As they sat on the side benches unlacing their skates after an hour of skating, Tyler said, "I'm hungry again. How about having dinner with me? I know a fantastic country-style restaurant, and it's a nice drive."

"All we seem to do when I'm with you is eat!" laughed Robbie. "What are you trying to do? Ply me with food?"

"Whatever it takes." Tyler's eyes twinkled.

They left the skating rink and walked out into the bright winter sunshine to Tyler's parked car.

After the long stretch of chill, damp weather, the day seemed gloriously bright and clear. Even in late afternoon the sky was a brilliant blue. Tyler had pressed the button to roll back the car's top. Robbie breathed in the tangy scent of the air and enjoyed the crisp snap of wind blowing back her hair as the open car zoomed along the interstate.

After they had left the freeway and were driving along the less traveled country roads, they saw that there were still fall colors on some of the trees flanking the old highway. Robbie felt absurdly young and free and happy.

As they drove along, Tyler suddenly looked over at her with a puzzled smile and declared, "You know, I haven't spent this much time with the same girl since I was in college. You must be something special."

At his words, Robbie felt her heart take flight like a balloon soaring into the sky. She could not think of anything to say, so she just looked back at him. He reached over and took her hand, releasing it only to shift gears.

Some time later, Tyler swerved off onto a side road, and they drove a little farther on what appeared to be a winding private driveway. At the end stood a sprawling white clapboard and stone farmhouse with a circling verandah etched against the December sky. "This is it!" he said, stopping the car.

"It looks like somebody's grandmother's house," Robbie remarked. "I love it!"

"Good! Wait until you taste the food!"

Out of the sun it felt suddenly cold. Robbie shivered in spite of her wool plaid pants and deep green sweater. Tyler put his arm around her shoulders as they walked up to the house. "You'll be warm in a minute," he promised.

He was right. Once they stepped inside they were enveloped by the cozy warmth of the place. A smiling hostess led them into a room where a welcoming fire burned merrily in a stone fireplace with a raised hearth. A large comfortable sofa was drawn up in front of it.

"We can have our drinks in here," Tyler said. "Two hot spiced ciders," he told the hostess. He looked at Robbie, lifted one eyebrow, and grinned. "See what a good influence you are?" In the coppery glow from the firelight, Tyler's eyes seemed to soften as they rested on Robbie for a long moment.

With their cider in hand, they surveyed the menu. Since dinner was served farm style, they had their choice of one of three entrées. The rest of the meal consisted of vegetables in season, rice, hot biscuits, cornbread, salad, and homemade pies a la mode.

"*My* grandmother never served such a menu!" exclaimed Robbie, remembering her remark about the place looking like somebody's grandmother's house. "Did yours?"

"No." Tyler shook his head. "In fact, my grandmother didn't cook very well at all."

They both laughed and then sat watching the fire in a kind of companionable contentment, until their waitress came to say their dinner was ready to be served.

Tyler put down his cider, took Robbie's hand, and said, "This has been a very special day." She looked up into his fine, lean face searchingly. His expression was serious as he returned her intent gaze. Was this, after all, a man she could trust—trust with her heart, her love, her life?

They lingered over coffee after dinner, but their conversation was sporadic. It kept drifting off distractedly as they looked into each other's eyes over the flickering light of the small hurricane lamp on the table. Time seemed magically suspended and unhurried.

Tyler reached across the table and took her hand, bringing it up to his lips. "Happy?" he asked her.

"Yes." Robbie nodded, her heart too full to add that she felt happier than she could ever remember.

At last, Tyler regretfully mentioned that he had an early flight the next day and it was time to go.

"Wait a minute," he said to Robbie before they went outside. "I'll be right back."

He came back carrying his sheepskin-lined suede car coat. "It's such a beautiful night, I thought we'd leave the top down—that is, if you won't be too cold. I brought this to wrap you up in." He grinned. "It will swallow you, but it will keep you snug and warm."

He had an extra sweater for himself in the car. As she snuggled into the seat beside him, with the wooly collar turned up over her ears, Robbie's spirits were high. With Tyler there was always some unexpected experience.

The powerful motor of the sports car purred as they started back to town. Robbie put her head back against the leather seat and gazed up at the clear winter sky far overhead. It was a dark velvet infinity sprinkled with thousands of stars glistening like sequins.

Their goodnight was brief, ending with a light kiss. As Tyler ran down the steps from the little deck of Robbie's new apartment, he called back, "I'll call you!"

And this time she was sure he would.

Robbie got ready for bed slowly, almost dreamily. She sensed that today had been a sort of turning point. She and Tyler had spent *hours* together, and it had been wonderful—no strain, no pressure, no tension. Who would have imagined it?

All she had heard about him before she met him, and then her own bad impression, gradually had faded and been proven untrue as she had come to know him.

He had told her she was "special." What did being "special" mean to someone like Tyler Lang? Was this all just the novelty of a new challenge for him? He made a girl feel that there was no one else in the room—in the world, for that matter. He was dangerously seductive. It would be so easy to believe she really *was* special to him—easy to fall in love with him. But it had been easy for other girls before her.

Robbie brushed her hair vigorously until her scalp tingled. With each stroke she told herself that it would be a mistake for her to take everything that Tyler said seriously. Foolish to think he was not playing his familiar line as cleverly with her as he had with others. Maybe for some girls it would not be so important. But for her, given what she knew she wanted in a relationship, it would be a terrible mistake.

And I'm not going to make that mistake, Robbie told herself. *I'd better back off a little—not accept the next date. It's all going too fast too soon.*

She opened the bedroom and stood breathing in the sharp, cold night air and looking out at the still star-studded sky. It had been a magical evening, but she could not let herself be fooled by T. J. Lang's brand of magic.

Chapter Ten

In the next few days Robbie discovered that slowing down the momentum of a romance is easier said than done. On the Monday after their Christmas shopping excursion, an enormous crimson poinsettia plant from Tyler was delivered. She opened the card and smiled as she read his enclosed note.

When she phoned to thank him, he said, "I was going to send you a partridge in a pear tree, but I couldn't figure how to manage the lords a' leaping and the maids a' milking."

Robbie giggled. "Thank goodness for that. How would I ever explain all that commotion to my landlady?"

"I've always tried to figure out how that legendary fellow did it anyway. And what did his true love do with all that loot after it arrived?" Tyler went on. "By the way, did I thank you for your expertise in dissolving all my Christmas problems? I woke up Sunday morning wondering why I felt so good, and then I remembered why."

"Yes, you did thank me—more than adequately, and the poinsettia is really lovely," Robbie told him.

"By the way, since you love ballet, would you be interested in seeing *The Nutcracker?* There's a matinee on the twenty-fourth."

"Oh, Tyler, I thought you knew I'm scheduled to fly on the twenty-fourth, twenty-fifth, and twenty-sixth," Robbie said regretfully.

"You *are*? I get in the night of the twenty-third. I thought maybe we could spend Christmas Eve—at least a part of it—together." There was genuine disappointment in his voice.

"Will you be here for Christmas?" she asked.

"No. Actually, I'm planning to fly down to Florida the evening of the twenty-fourth. We're—my family—spending Christmas with my grandmother. I'm not sure she wants us, but my mother insists we go. She called and reminded me Gran will be seventy-two next year and *you never know!* Of course, that's what Mom always says. *Last* year she laid on the guilt by saying Gran would be *seventy-one!* Robbie, my grandmother is the youngest person in our entire family! I mean it. She swims every day, rides a bike, and has a very active social life. I predict Gran will outlive us all. And who knows? We may be ruining some plans she has of her own for the holiday when we arrive en masse."

"Oh, maybe not. Don't you think she'll enjoy it?"

"I guess so. We'll all probably eat too much and sit around watching a football game on TV. My brother-in-law and Dad are sports nuts—that is *spectator* sports nuts. I'll try to get in some surfing. But it's not much of a way to spend Christmas."

When she hung up Robbie thought there had been some hidden element in their conversation, something she could not quite put her finger on, something in Tyler's tone of voice. It was almost as if he wanted her to suggest some way for them to be together. It kept nagging at her for definition. She tried to dismiss it as her imagination. Surely, the plans she had for the next few days would seem corny to the sophisticated T. J. Lang.

Robbie loved Christmas more than any other holiday. She enjoyed everything about it, the undercurrent of excitement, the dazzling displays in store windows, the lights, decorations, and the music. She even liked the things other people found chores—the shopping, sending cards, searching for just the right gifts. She had grown up in a home with cherished holiday traditions, and even when she could not make it home for Christmas, she clung to the well-loved rituals.

Robbie did most of her actual shopping on layovers, but she saved the wrapping to do all at once while she listened to familiar carols on her stereo or radio. Her mood of anticipation started early and grew steadily the closer Christmas came.

Since she had to fly on the holiday itself, the few days beforehand she spent doing the things she most enjoyed. One morning she went browsing in the mini-mall not far from her apartment. Although she didn't like the panic of last-minute shopping, she liked mingling in the holiday crowds, gazing at the gorgeous gift arrays in the stores, and experiencing the sights and sounds of Christmas in the air.

As she walked through the arcade of the mall and heard the carillon playing, mixed with the ringing of the Salvation Army bell and the happy voices of children lined up for a visit with the department store Santa, Robbie felt caught up in the whole atmosphere of this special time of year. The only thing missing was someone to share it with, and for a minute she had a little twinge of loneliness.

She wandered through a card-and-candle shop picking out special gift tags for each member of her family and then selected several rolls of colorful wrapping paper, ribbons of various colors, stickers, and tape. She could not choose between two fragrantly scented candles and ended up buying both.

On her way home Robbie passed the Community Church and heard the ringing voices of their choir rehearsing for the Christmas services. She slipped inside and found a seat in one of the back pews of the darkened interior. Only the choir loft was lighted, and as the sound of "O Holy Night" rose in majesty and power, Robbie felt a little tingle along her spine. "A thrill of hope, the weary world rejoices. . . ." The triumphant words rang high into the raftered ceiling and filled Robbie with a joyous and childlike expectancy at this celebration of Christ's birth.

Christmas is such a wonderful time, she thought. Christmas alone or Christmas, flying, it didn't make any difference—she was going to celebrate it with a full heart!

She had not planned to have a tree, but impulsively she decided to buy one on her way home. After all, it was her first Christmas in her very own place, and she could have any kind of Christmas she chose—and she chose to have an old-fashioned one.

Robbie drove to the nursery and picked a small shapely pine already attached to a stand. When she placed it in the corner of her tiny living room she felt festive rather than foolish. She would trim it with strings of popcorn, cranberries and homemade cookies!

Just as she had finished getting out the ingredients for sugar cookies, a knock came at her front door.

It was Mrs. Holmes, and when Robbie opened the door for her, Cyrano slipped into the apartment, meowing loudly and rubbing against Robbie's legs.

Mrs. Holmes clucked her tongue and shook her head. "Naughty cat! He was just waiting for his chance. You see I'm going away to spend Christmas with my sister in Decatur, and he always seems to sense when I'm leaving. Thinks he'll find himself another place to stay."

Robbie bent down and scooped Cyrano up in her arms, nuzzling her chin against his soft, furry head.

"He's welcome, Mrs. Holmes. Although I'll be away myself most of Christmas Eve, all day Christmas, and part of the next day. But it's okay for now."

"Well, if you're sure," Mrs. Holmes said doubtfully. "I have one of those automatic feeding stations for my cats for both their food and water, so they have everything they need. And I'll only be gone overnight. . . ."

"It will be fine for Cyrano to stay here, really!" Robbie assured her as Cyrano began to purr contentedly.

"I've brought you one of my fruitcakes, Robbie," Mrs. Holmes said handing her a package wrapped in shiny green cellophane topped with a sprig of holly. "I hope you'll have a Merry Christmas, dear."

"You, too, Mrs. Holmes. Have a nice time with your sister, and thanks very much for the fruitcake," Robbie called after her as she went down the porch steps.

Robbie poured some whipping cream into a saucer for Cyrano. While he was happily lapping it up, she tied a red ribbon around his neck and attached a tiny sleigh bell, so that whenever he moved, it made a merry jingle.

She went back to reading the recipe card and making sure she had everything she needed for her cookies. Then the phone rang.

"What are you doing this afternoon?" It was Tyler.

"I don't know whether you're ready for this," Robbie replied hesitantly.

"Try me."

"I'm baking Christmas cookies."

"Mmmm. Sounds great." He paused, then said, "*Quaint*—but great!" Tyler's rich, deep laugh came rolling over the phone.

Robbie smiled in spite of herself.

Then Tyler asked, "Need any help?"

Again Robbie hesitated, but there was a note of eagerness in his voice she could not resist.

"Sure!" she said. All her resolutions about *not* seeing him so often faded away at the very thought of *seeing* him!

"You mean it?"

"Yes."

"Want me to bring anything . . . like sugar plums or—?"

"*Tyler!*" Robbie laughed.

"Okay! Just trying to get into the Christmas spirit."

"Good, just bring that."

Robbie was sliding her first tray of cookies out of the oven when Tyler rapped at the door. The whole apartment was fragrant with delicious baking smells as he walked in with a large paper sack in each arm.

"What in the world!" Robbie exclaimed. "I told you not to bring anything!"

"Oh, I just thought of a couple of things that might be fun. 'Tis the season to be jolly and all that." He grinned as he set down the brown grocery bags on the counter divider and began unloading them. A carton of eggnog, some mocha-mint ice cream, a frozen mince pie, a quart of cranberry juice, and some frozen lemonade. From the second bag he drew out a sprig of mistletoe.

"Where shall I hang this?" he demanded. Then leaning across the counter, he dangled it over Robbie's head and suggested, "After testing it first, of course!" He kissed her lightly on the lips.

He pulled one of the kitchen stools to the center of the room, climbed up, and tied the mistletoe on the overhead light. Then he stood, hands on his hips, and looked around the apartment.

Following his glance, Robbie saw how cluttered the place was with the boxes and packages containing the presents she planned to wrap that evening, along with her new purchases of wrapping paper and ribbon she had dumped on the sofa when she came home.

"This looks like the annex to Neiman Marcus," Tyler declared. He picked up the fluffy, honey-brown teddy bear. "Who is this for?"

"That's for Tessa, my girlfriend's little girl."

"Are you sure you're not somehow related to Santa Claus? I never saw anyone so crazy about buying Christmas presents—not that I don't appreciate your skill. I certainly took advantage of it," he commented. Approaching the kitchen he started rolling up his sleeves and said, "Now, show me what to do."

Tyler proved surprisingly adept at cutting out cookies and seemed thoroughly to enjoy decorating them. Robbie was cleaning up the pans and bowls and wiping off the counters when Tyler announced, "Now, it's my turn. I have a neat recipe for a hot, *nonalcoholic* drink. It's one of those bits of irrelevant, odd pieces of information I picked up somewhere. I don't remember how I got it or who gave it to me. I just know it tastes great. Have you got a saucepan around here?"

"Of course!" Robbie said with mock indignation. "This is a very well-equipped kitchen!" She got one out and handed it to him.

"I should never have questioned that. My apologies!" Tyler placed a hand abjectly on his chest and bowed his head. "Now, watch carefully—to one quart of cranberry juice, you add a can of frozen lemonade, a teaspoon of cinnamon, that is if you don't happen to have 'mulling spices'? No? Well then, a pinch of ginger and nutmeg, allow to simmer, then serve."

Later, as they sat on the sofa sipping the delightfully spicy mixture, Robbie smiled at Tyler and said, "You are full of surprises!"

"So are *you*," he retorted. His eyes filled with tender amusement as he glanced around the gaily decorated apartment.

Outside it had begun to rain in the early dusk. The sound of it pebbling against the windowpanes and the glow of the small twinkling lights Tyler had helped Robbie thread through the branches of the little tree combined to give them a feeling of warmth and intimacy. Robbie's mind suddenly flashed on how it might be if they . . . but then she pushed the thought away. This afternoon had been a novel experience for Tyler—something completely out of character, she felt sure. This kind of domesticity would bore him eventually. He had all but told her that. But, right now, he seemed perfectly relaxed and completely enjoying himself.

Around five the paperboy knocked on the door to hand Robbie her evening news and receive in return a big package with a glossy bow.

"Gifts for the paperboy, too?" Tyler raised his eyebrows.

"A model plane. He loves models," she said shyly.

"You are something else," Tyler remarked slowly. He took the paper from her and opened it, glancing at the headlines and turning the pages. Then he exclaimed, "Guess what's on TV tonight?"

"What?"

"Dickens's *A Christmas Carol.* Want to watch?"

So Tyler was planning to stay on through the evening? Robbie mused. She covered her surprise and answered, "Sounds like a reasonable idea for a few days before Christmas."

They made omelets, baked the mince pie, popped popcorn, and ate it in front of the TV set as the familiar, beloved story played out on the screen.

When the movie ended with the exuberant Scrooge dancing a jig and wishing everyone in sight a Merry Christmas, Tyler stretched and sighed and got to his feet. "I guess I better go and let you get some sleep."

He took Robbie's hand, and she walked with him to the door. Before they reached it, he stopped and pulled her close. He looked above where they were standing and said softly, "You're standing under the mistletoe." He put a hand under her chin and tilted it up. "Not that I need an excuse." Then he kissed her—a longer kiss this time than a casual seasonal greeting.

When he released her he spoke in a low voice, "It's been a fantastic day, Robbie. But then . . . with you, it's always special."

At the door he said, "I almost forgot. I've got something for you to open before you leave on flight Christmas Day."

He ran down the outside steps and out to his car. In a matter of minutes he was back with a deep, rectangular package beautifully wrapped in gold foil and a lavish crimson bow.

Robbie was a little flustered. She had debated about getting him a gift, and then decided it might not be appropriate. Now, she wished she had something for him, even something small.

He lingered a little longer, as if trying to make up his mind about something. "By the way, I meant to ask. Do you have any ghosts of Christmas Past lurking in the background? Any old haunting memories of lost loves?"

"Are you serious?" Robbie asked amazed.

"Yes." His tone was even, although his eyes were twinkling.

Slowly Robbie shook her head.

"Good!" Tyler said with satisfaction. He leaned down and kissed her again. Then he was gone.

Christmas morning Robbie heard the sound of steady rain before she opened her eyes. She lay there listening to it for several minutes longer, playing with the vain hope that the storm might be bad enough to cancel her flight. But the dull beat of a steady drizzle continued, and she finally reached out to flip on her bedside radio. Immediately the lyrics of the perennial popular melody sung by the familiar crooner poured into the room.

"*Wet* not *white*," she mumbled as she tossed back the covers and padded into the bathroom to shower. Emerging, now wide awake, she realized that it was Christmas and she had Tyler's present to open before she left for the airport.

The package was almost too pretty to open, she thought as she carefully loosened the ribbon and slid her fingers under the taped corners of the gold paper. She lifted the lid of the box, pushed aside the sheaves of tissue paper, and her hands felt the smooth richness of fine leather. She brought out a finely crafted, navy blue handbag with an adjustable strap. Inside the beautifully finished interior she found three small wrapped gifts: a wallet with her initials in gold, a small spray bottle of her favorite scent, and a lovely silk designer scarf. The present was in perfect taste. Tyler had managed to strike just the right note—a gift that showed individualized thoughtfulness without being presumptively personal.

The terminal was nearly deserted as Robbie walked through on her way to Operations to sign in at Crew Scheduling.

"Not much of a payload," growled Captain Larson as he came on board. "Not good for my Trans-Continent stock." He looked morose but gave Robbie a wink as he passed her on his way into the cockpit. She had flown with Carl Larson before, and she knew he was all bark and no bite. His copilot, Second Officer Cliff Farnsworth, was a different story. "Bring me up some coffee as soon as you can," he grumbled as he went by. "Why would anyone want to fly anywhere on Christmas Day anyhow? There oughta be a law against it."

"And Merry Christmas to you, too!" Robbie's fellow flight attendant said in a low voice behind Farnsworth's departing back. Then she smiled at Robbie. "Anyway, there's a full turkey dinner to serve. That ought to cheer him up."

Robbie looked over the passenger manifest and saw Captain Larson was right. There were only a few passengers, which meant low revenues, hardly worth the price of the jet fuel for the trip. But one bright note was that they could give more personalized attention when there were fewer passengers to serve.

As it turned out, the flight was smooth and for some reason all the passengers on board that day were pleasant. She and Christy were able to work the flight easily and enjoy it. Even Farnsworth became more cheerful. By the time the return flight landed back in Atlanta, Robbie realized Christmas Day had passed without a touch of homesickness or heartache.

After filing her flight log, she passed through the airport lobby and glanced at the row of clocks along the wall showing the time in different national and international zones. How lovely to think that all around the world Christmas was being celebrated. In the Philippines it had just begun. People were returning from midnight church services. In Alaska little children were just waking up to find what Santa had left for them. In England people were having a holiday tea. Here, her own family was probably gathering around the table to sit down for the traditional turkey dinner. And in the Holy Land, it was evening, the stars in the dark sky reminding people of that first star-bright night in Bethlehem.

As she drove home through the gathering darkness of the misty, rainy afternoon, Robbie passed house after house whose uncurtained windows showed scenes of decorated trees, doors opening to arriving guests. Strangely enough, it did not make her feel lonely. Christmas was so much more than shop windows, the tinsel, lights, and certainly more than presents, which were only a symbol of the real gift of Christmas, Jesus' birth. She smiled to herself with a happy lifting of her heart, knowing that in spite of having to fly, this had been a very special Christmas.

Chapter Eleven

"When will you be back?" Tyler asked, frowning. He and Robbie were sitting in the airport coffee shop. Taped Christmas music played in the background, and the hum of conversation was louder than usual in the room full of holiday travelers.

Robbie replied, "It depends. I have five days off, but I'll be flying nonrevenue-seat-available, so I can't be sure. I should be back on the first."

"Non-rev is always chancy." Tyler shook his head scowling. "Especially now."

"But between Christmas and New Year's most people are at the destination where they want to be and haven't started home yet."

"I still wish you weren't going," he said.

"But my family is counting on it. They saved their Christmas so that I could be with them, since I was scheduled to fly the twenty-fourth through the twenty-sixth and couldn't make it home then."

"I wanted you to spend New Year's Eve with me."

"You better not plan on it."

"I wish I'd known," Tyler grumbled. "I could have come back a day sooner, and we could have celebrated early."

Robbie smiled. "I'm sorry," she said, thinking how handsome he looked. His tan had deepened to a ruddy bronze from his vacation in Florida, and his hair was tousled and longer than he usually wore it. The bright blue and red of his Norwegian sweater gave him a rugged, outdoorsy look.

Just moments before, they had run into each other in the crowded terminal lobby. Tyler was returning from Florida, and Robbie was about to leave for a belated Christmas with her family.

They looked at each other. They had not seen each other for nearly a week. Tyler's eyes moved over her as if memorizing each detail. She seemed prettier than ever to him, in a soft, pale blue, cowl-necked sweater, with her hair in coppery little swirls. Tiny gold hoops dangled from her small shell-pink ears.

They both started to say something but were interrupted by the blare of the public address system announcing Robbie's plane. She grabbed her camel-hair coat and reached for her cordovan-brown leather bag. "I'll have to go."

"I'll walk you to the gate," Tyler said, taking her arm.

They reached the sign that read PASSENGERS ONLY BEYOND THIS POINT, and she turned toward him. Tyler had pulled her near for a kiss when he was hailed by two fellow pilots coming through the arrivals gate. They stopped to ask him how Florida had been. After that there was only time to say good-bye before Robbie hurried to pass through the security check.

She turned to wave and Tyler called, "Let me know when you get back!" She nodded, waved again, and then disappeared around the corner of the corridor to the loading bridge.

The Mallory family's delayed Christmas was festive and fun. Robbie's time at home was filled with family and friends, visits and visiting. She did all the traditional things they had always done, enjoying it all, and yet there seemed to be something missing. There was a tiny part of her that was not participating as completely as she had in the past. There was a longing little ache in her heart because she was not sharing this holiday with someone who, she realized, was becoming very important to her.

Too important? Robbie often wondered that during her days at home. And even if Tyler were here with her, how would he feel about the homey things that were a part of who she was? Would the Mallorys' simple, small town, family-oriented lifestyle seem somehow corny to his worldly taste?

Robbie did not have a lot of time to think about this or even about Tyler, for that matter. Her days were too crammed with people, outings, hometown events, neighborhood parties, and open houses—that is, until New Year's Eve and the watch night services at the church she had attended all her life.

Robbie's mother asked her father to go with them, as she did each year, and he said no in his usual nice but firm reply. Robbie saw the wistfulness in her mother's face and the lurking sadness in her eyes as she turned away. Something cold pinched Robbie's heart at what she observed. That's the way it was when your faith in Christ is not shared, she realized.

She did not want to think about it, but somehow that little scene between her parents kept thrusting itself back into her mind all through the service.

The church was still decorated for Christmas with the tall Christmas tree standing at one side of the altar, banks of red poinsettia, garlands of natural greenery draped over each window, and lighted candles burning in each windowsill.

As the service moved from one part to the next, each pointing to the new year ahead, Robbie's thoughts turned to Tyler. She knew deep in her heart that the more she was with Tyler, the more she wanted to be with him. All the myths about love made sense to her now; all the lyrics of romantic ballads seemed to have been written specifically about her feelings. She knew that she and T. J. were on the brink of something. They had come to a turning point in their relationship where a choice of some kind would have to be made.

Lord, what should I do? Robbie prayed. *Is it right for us to go on? Is Tyler who you want for me? Help me to know,* she pleaded.

The congregation rose to sing a familiar old hymn, "Trust and Obey." Although Robbie had not heard it recently, she had known the words since childhood.

Trust and obey,
For there's no other way
To be happy in Jesus
But to trust and obey.

Even as she sang Robbie was praying, *I'll try to do that, Lord—trust that you'll show me the way.*

As the pastor prepared to dismiss them, he said, "There are still some little Scripture verses on the tree. If anyone did not get one on Christmas, please take one before you leave."

It was a custom in their church to tie small slips of paper sealed with red tags on the tree. Each slip contained a Bible quotation to be used as a special Scripture for the coming year. As a child, Robbie had always loved the suspense of opening the slip and reading her special verse.

As they rose to leave the service, she asked her mother to wait while she went up and pulled one of the last few slips from the tree. She did not have a chance to open it until she was back in her old room and ready to get into bed.

Curious, she tore open the red tag, took out the slip of paper, and read

Trust in the LORD. . . .
Delight yourself also in the LORD,
And He shall give you the desires of your heart.
Commit your way to the LORD,
Trust also in Him,
And He shall bring it to pass. Psalm 37:3, 4, 5.

That's my answer! Robbie thought.

She had to leave early the next morning to catch the first flight out, which usually was not as crowded as the later ones. It was a relief to have no trouble getting a seat. She got on board, settled into a seat, and tucked a pillow behind her head, preparing to sleep all the way back to Atlanta. She was scheduled to work a later flight that day and needed to rest.

Her seat was in the rear of the plane near the galley, and she could not help overhearing the conversation between the two stewardesses working the flight. She had asked at the ticket counter who would be working the flight but did not know either of them. Robbie was half drowsing and not even conscious of listening, but she came wide awake when she heard the name *Tyler Lang.*

"I hear he's off the available list," one of the stews said.

"How so?"

"New interest."

"Oh, that! Give him another few weeks."

"The word is that it's already lasted two months."

"Well—" the other girl's drawn-out reply was underlined with doubt. "I've never known his flings to last over six weeks at the longest."

"Want to bet?"

"I'd be crazy to at those odds."

They both laughed and went on to another subject.

All her life, Robbie had heard the expression, "eavesdroppers never hear well of themselves." As her ears actually began to tingle, she realized it must be true. She slid further down in her seat, even though the two stewardesses could not possibly know that she was the subject they had been discussing. She hated the thought of being a topic of gossip.

It was raining when the plane landed in Atlanta, and Robbie took a cab out to her apartment.

As she unlocked the door and went in, the phone was ringing. She set down her suitcase and started to run to pick it up. Suddenly there was a knock at the front door. She stood in the middle of her small living room for a moment, undecided which to answer first.

The knock sounded insistent. Hopefully whoever was on the phone would hold on or call back, Robbie reasoned fleetingly as she hurried to open the door.

A huge cluster of brightly colored balloons filled the doorway. As she gazed in stunned amazement, the smiling face of a clown peeked around one side.

"Holiday delivery!" he chirped in a high, funny voice. "Happy New Year, Roblynn Mallory!"

Robbie had to hold onto the door frame she was laughing so hard. "How wonderful!" she exclaimed. "Thank you!"

"Here's the sender's card!" the clown said, thrusting the bunch of balloons and a card at her.

The phone continued ringing. Robbie had a little trouble pulling the floating balloons into the apartment and closing the door. Still holding onto the strings, she rushed over to grab the phone and said breathlessly, "Hello!"

"You're back!" It was Tyler, sounding elated.

"Yes, I'm back and being attacked by a bunch of balloons that some crazy person sent me!" she laughed helplessly.

She could hear Tyler chuckling. "So! You're the kind of woman who attracts weird men!" he teased. "Have you eaten breakfast?"

"No, I'm barely awake. I was at the airport before six this morning," she said.

"Good! I'm taking you to brunch at Brennan's. I'll be over in fifteen minutes."

"But, I just got in. . . ."

"I *know*. I want to see you. I've got to leave in three hours on a flight. I'll be right over."

"This doesn't quite make up for New Year's Eve," Tyler said, holding up his orange juice glass and clicking its rim with Robbie's raised one, as they sat at a corner table at the popular restaurant in Buckhead.

"Was it fun?" Robbie asked. "Your New Year's Eve?"

"Not much. Believe it or not, I went home before midnight." He helped himself to a generous dollop of sour cream for his strawberry crepes. "How about yours? What did you do? Go out with your old hometown boyfriend?" Tyler's voice was casual, but he was eyeing Robbie sharply.

She hesitated a moment. Should she tell him how she had spent New Year's Eve? Would he possibly understand? Well, if they were going to go on together, everything should be out in the open about each other. Robbie replied, "No. I went to church."

Tyler, his coffee cup in hand and halfway to his mouth, halted. Something curious flickered in the depths of his eyes as he stared at her, startled. "*Church*?" he repeated, as if he had not quite heard her correctly.

Robbie felt herself blush under his penetrating gaze. "Yes. We always go. It's a good way to start the New Year, don't you think?"

"I don't know. I guess so. I mean, if that's your thing," Tyler said, shrugging slightly.

The waitress came to refill their coffee cups and the awkward moment passed. Robbie had hoped that Tyler would ask her more about the service, what it was like, and why her family always went. But he didn't. To bridge the gap that seemed to have opened between them, Robbie asked, "Where is your flight today? You didn't say where you were going this afternoon."

"I hate to tell you," he said with a little smile. "It's Bermuda. I wish you were going along." He paused, then asked, "Anything you'd like me to bring back for you?"

"A handful of pink coral sand!" She looked into his eyes, wondering if that day at the cove was as cherished a memory to him as it was to her.

"You got it!" He smiled back at her and her heart thumped wildly. *Oh, Lord,* she prayed inwardly, *please let it work out. I really do want him to love me.*

"Ready?" Tyler asked. They got up to leave.

Since he had to go straight to the airport, he dropped her off in front of the house. Before she got out, he put his arm around her and drew her close. Her mouth yielded to the sweetness of his long, lingering kiss. When it ended he said huskily, "Did I tell you that I missed you?"

"And I missed you," she whispered.

She stood at the curb and watched the shiny black sportscar pull away and streak into the road toward the freeway. She felt somehow forlorn, not knowing when their schedules would permit them to be in town at the same time again.

Chapter Twelve

To Robbie's surprise and delight, she found a note from Tyler in her airport mailbox when she returned from her first flight of the new year.

I'm back! If it's not too last-minute, can we have dinner Saturday night? Call if you can't make it.

TJL

As she dressed for the evening on Saturday, Robbie felt like a schoolgirl before her first prom. She was ready a full forty-five minutes before Tyler was to come and kept running out on the deck, peering anxiously to see if his car were pulling into the driveway!

Her cheeks were flushed and her eyes were bright with anticipation of the evening ahead—their first since Ty's Bermuda trip. At last she heard the sound of the motor of the black sportscar and ducked into her bedroom to take a last-minute look at herself. She was wearing a dress she had found at one of the fabulous after-Christmas sales. It was made of crushed velvet the color of cinnamon with a V neckline, wide cummerbund waist, and flared skirt. Deep ruffles of ecru lace fell gracefully over her wrists. She adored the color and the old-fashioned effect of the style and fabric. Satisfied, Robbie whirled around and dashed into the living room. She opened the front door just as Tyler raised his hand to knock.

There was a split-second hesitation as he looked at her. Then, he said in an awed voice, "If you aren't a picture! I'm almost afraid to kiss you—you might not be real."

"I'm real," Robbie assured him, stepping closer and putting her arms around his neck.

They kissed, tentatively at first, then a longer, sweetly satisfying kiss. When it ended, Robbie was shaken to a tingling depth.

She shivered a little at the cold wind sweeping in from the porch. "Come in," she said softly, taking his hand and gently pulling him inside.

Tyler's broad-shouldered height seemed to fill the small living room as he stood, hands in his pockets. "Your place looks nice," he remarked, looking around. "You've been doing some decorating, haven't you?"

"I guess a little since you were here last. I've acquired a few new things," Robbie answered.

Robbie liked color, and she had replaced the rather drab beige curtains with some bright rust woven ones, hung some new plants, and tossed several large pillows in yellow, burnt orange, and green onto the studio couch. Along the top of the bookcase which she had made from boards and ornamental cement blocks were three clay pots of bronze, yellow and white chrysanthemums—*and Cyrano.*

Spotting the lazy feline, Tyler chuckled. "Among the new things, a *cat*?"

"Oh, that's Cyrano, one of Mrs. Holmes's cats. He's sort of adopted me or vice versa. Mrs. Holmes has three cats, and the Persian has just had kittens, so I think Cyrano felt a little shunted aside."

"Does he come up here to sulk or to be pampered?"

Robbie laughed. "Both, probably. I'm almost ready. Would you like a cup of coffee or something?" she asked.

"No thanks. I'll wait. No hurry."

"I won't be a minute," she said and disappeared into the bedroom to get her coat and purse.

When she returned, he was sitting on the couch, leaning over the coffee table, where her magazines and books were spread. He held up the book he had in his hands, raised his eyebrows, and remarked quizzically, "Jane Austen?"

Robbie felt herself blush and said defensively, "It's considered a classic, you know."

"A classic, yes. But hardly light reading for a modern young woman." He smiled, eyeing her with a puzzled interest.

"Well, I have to admit, it's the second time around. It was required reading in high school, and I think there's a danger in reading something like *Pride and Prejudice* too soon. Actually, I saw part of a dramatization of it on TV that sparked my interest. So I thought I'd give it another try."

"And—?"

"I'm enjoying it. In fact, I *like* it." She lifted her chin assertively, as if to justify her taste in reading.

"Don't be so defensive!" Tyler teased her, laughing. "I think that's marvelous. In a way, you're a good deal like Elizabeth Bennet."

"How do you mean?" she asked, surprised that he was familiar with the characters of this classic novel.

"You're not of your time," he answered enigmatically. "Elizabeth did not fit neatly into the slot of young ladies of *her* day either."

Not knowing exactly how to respond to his observation, Robbie said nothing. But she could not help thinking that Tyler's having read *Pride and Prejudice* revealed an unsuspected facet of his own personality.

He put the book down on the coffee table and got to his feet. "Ready to go?"

She handed him her dark brown velour coat and he helped her on with it. His hands lingered a moment on her shoulders and then touched the nape of her neck where her soft curls clustered.

"I've just thought of the perfect place to take you for dinner tonight," he announced, smiling down at her and tucking her arm through his.

The Mansion was a magnificent old Victorian home, restored and transformed into an elegant restaurant. They went up a curved, carpeted stairway into a room charmingly decorated in keeping with the era. Robbie admired the rose-patterned wallpaper, illuminated softly, as if by gaslight, from frilled, frosted lamps. She and T. J. were seated in a windowed alcove, overlooking an old-fashioned garden subtly lighted at night and shadowed by towering elms. There was starched white linen on the table and a single, fresh rose in a crystal vase in the center.

"Is this Victorian enough for you?" Tyler asked, his eyes snapping with pleasure at her delight in the atmosphere.

"It's lovely."

"It becomes you. The ideal background, straight out of a Jane Austen novel!" he declared with teasing affection.

Dinner complemented the ambiance of the place. A crisp salad was followed by an expertly poached salmon filet. Tyler had a glass of Chenin blanc, while Robbie sipped a chilled sparkling grape juice. Lime sherbet with wafer-thin cookies was dessert. Finally they were brought delicious, dark coffee in delicate demitasse cups.

Back in Tyler's car, after dinner, he said, "I almost forgot. I brought you something back from Bermuda. We'll go by my place to get it."

Robbie felt a small shiver of apprehension. She had never gone to Tyler's apartment in the fashionable high-rise condominium. Now she wondered if it would be wise to do so. But the vague uneasiness she felt came and went so quickly she was scarcely aware of it—not when going there meant prolonging her time with Tyler.

He slid the long, low sportscar into the space marked "T. J. Lang" in the underground parking garage. He got out, came around the car, and opened the other door for Robbie. With his arm around her waist they walked to the self-operated elevator. As the doors slid shut, Tyler smiled at Robbie and pushed the LOBBY button.

The lobby was large and luxuriously decorated with tropical plants and huge modern paintings. A security guard tipped his uniform cap and said, "Evening, Captain," and nodded to Robbie.

An unwanted thought slipped through her mind. *How many other young women has the man seen Tyler bring in here?* She brushed it aside.

After another elevator ride, doors opening onto a carpeted foyer, and a few yards down a wide hall, Tyler took out his key and opened the door to his place.

"Here we go," he said, stepping back so that she could precede him.

Robbie drew in her breath as she walked inside. Behind her, Tyler snapped on a wall switch that brought

111

the place into subtly lighted view. Robbie saw herself reflected in the mirrored walls as she looked around.

As he turned on the lights, dance music began playing! Robbie turned to Tyler questioningly. He smiled. "I fixed it so the hall lights activate my stereo. I hate coming into an empty, silent place," he explained.

They went down deeply carpeted steps into the sunken living room. The room seemed circular in shape, but it was an illusion created by the huge, creamy, curved, contour sofa. In its crescent was a free form, glass-topped coffee table and handsome, black and brass lamps on either end.

"Come see my view—Atlanta at night," Tyler suggested as he drew back floor-length sheer curtains. Her footsteps made no noise on the thick, deep-green carpet as she walked over to stand beside him and look at the panorama of the lighted city spread out before them.

"It's gorgeous," Robbie breathed. "Just fabulous."

"That alone makes living here worth it," he commented.

"Is it far from the airport?" she asked, not having paid much attention as Tyler had driven them here.

"Only two blocks and I'm on I-75 right to the airport."

They stood there looking out at the lights, shimmering like strings of dazzling jewels in crisscross design against the dark blue velvet night. Then Tyler spoke very quietly. "You know that *feeling* just before take-off?" he asked.

Robbie nodded. "Yes, I know what you mean; I get it every time."

"Well, I'm getting it now." He smiled. "I feel like I'm forty thousand feet in the air."

Robbie forced a laugh. "We almost are!" Their eyes met and her heart soared.

With that he drew her into his arms and his lips found her mouth. When she tried to pull away, he held her tighter. His kiss was long and hard and had a certain determination. As he pressed her to himself, she felt a warmth suffuse her whole being, and her resistance weakened. She responded with a shuddering sigh. He kissed her closed eyes, then her mouth again and again. She wound her arms around him and held him as a rush of joy—an unspeakable, nameless happiness—surged through her.

The room spun around her. The music from the stereo seemed to rise and encircle them, blending its rhythmic beat with her wildly beating heart. Tyler kissed her again, and her response was instant as his sweet, deep kisses made her beg for more. Suddenly, she had the sensation of teetering on a precipice. . . .

With an effort, Robbie brought herself back to the present. Her hands gently pushed against his chest, and she pulled away from him.

"I think," she began breathlessly, "I think I'd better go."

She saw a lightning flash of anger in his eyes as he held her a minute longer before letting her go. He turned away and jerked the cord that slid the draperies back across the wall of glass, shutting out the view. "Wait! I'll get your gift," he said briskly and then crossed the living room and vanished into the hall.

Left alone, Robbie looked around, trying to imagine Tyler Lang living here. The quality of his taste was evident from the paintings, a wood sculpture on the stereo cabinet, and a mounted amethyst geode on the coffee table. A book on modern art and some current weekly news magazines were fanned out alongside it.

"Close your eyes and hold out your hands," Tyler's voice directed behind her. She turned around, her eyes tightly shut, holding up cupped hands.

She felt him approach her, the scent of his expensive cologne recognizable.

With a childlike anticipation, she exclaimed, "What is it?"

"What did you ask for?" he reminded her.

"A handful of pink coral sand from Bermuda," she answered. Then she felt the cool spill of—not sand—but something more like tiny jagged stones pour into her hands until they were full. "When can I open my eyes and look?"

"Now," Ty said.

Obeying him, Robbie looked down and saw a handful of lovely coral beads. She gave a soft cry of pleasure. "Oh, Ty! They're beautiful! Thank you. What a dear, thoughtful thing to do—to bring me back a piece of Bermuda!"

He took them from her and put them around her neck. His fingers on her bare skin as he clasped the necklace sent a delicious feeling of intimacy shivering through her.

He leaned close and kissed her cheek. "I wish I could take *you* back to Bermuda."

She turned to look up at him, wishing that he would add, "*on our honeymoon.*" They stood, inches apart, gazing at each other.

Robbie desperately wanted to say, "Tyler, I love you." But she wanted *him* to say it *first*, and he didn't. Instead he bent and kissed her lightly and said, "Well, I guess I'd better take you home."

Chapter Thirteen

"I've made all the arrangements," Tyler told her.

"But I don't ski!" protested Robbie.

"You'll learn! They have bunny slopes for beginners." Ty grinned. "There's no use making excuses. I'm not taking no for an answer. We'll leave first thing in the morning. It takes about five or six hours to drive up to Beech Mountain. We'll have the rest of tomorrow, all of the next day, and part of another. I know you're going to love it!" he declared.

Robbie was not that certain, but she wanted to please Tyler. She knew that it was important to share the things he liked to do with him. She had never been particularly athletic, but now she wanted to become a part of everything in his life. If skiing were a prerequisite, then she was willing to try.

"I'm not sure I have the right clothes," was Robbie's last weak protest.

"*Women!*" Ty struck his forehead in mock despair. "The resort is full of shops, and you can rent boots and ski equipment there. There's nothing for you to worry about, Robbie—nothing for you to do but relax and enjoy yourself!" he assured her laughingly.

Tyler had met Robbie's flight and driven her home. They stood on the deck outside her apartment door.

"Now are there any more unsettled questions?" he demanded, looking down at her, his eyes sparkling with amusement.

Robbie shook her head slowly.

"Good!" he declared decisively. "Just get a good night's sleep," and I'll be by to pick you up a little after seven, okay?"

"Okay." Robbie answered meekly.

Tyler bent down and kissed her—a warm, seeking kiss that lengthened possessively. Then he pulled her into his arms and held her tightly for a few minutes. "I can't wait to show you one of my favorite places and to show you off! Sweet dreams, sweetheart." After another light kiss he scampered down the porch steps whistling.

Robbie stirred sleepily, burrowing deeper into the blanket and pulling it over her head against the persistent sound of the phone. Gradually she came awake and groped with one hand for the bedside phone and fumbled for the receiver.

"This is your wake-up call," Tyler's brisk, alert voice announced.

Robbie muffled a groan.

"Come on!" he urged. "Up and at 'em. I'll be over in about forty-five minutes. Put some coffee on." There was a click and then the dial tone.

How did I ever get into this? Robbie asked herself as she dragged out of the temptingly warm bed, shuffled into the bathroom, and turned on the shower.

Nevertheless, when Tyler's familiar knock came at the front door, she was dressed and waiting. Tyler, handsome in a heavy, ribbed coat sweater, stepped inside, rubbing his hands together excitedly. His eyes, bright with anticipation, roved around the room eagerly.

116

"All set?" he asked, smiling broadly.

"As ready as I'll ever be, I guess," Robbie said doubtfully.

"Do I detect a note of hesitation?" Ty inquired playfully.

She shrugged. "Not really. I just hope my lack of skill on skis won't be a major disappointment to you."

"You serious?" Tyler looked at her sharply.

"Well, after all, this will be my first time on skis. . . ."

In a few quick strides, he went over to her and put his hands on her waist and drew her close. "Honey, it's not all that crucial! I just want you to enjoy the things I enjoy. I want us to do things together. I didn't want to go away on another ski trip without you. I don't expect you suddenly to be eligible for the Winter Olympics, for Pete's sake."

Robbie's heart felt its usual flutter at Tyler's nearness. She smiled up at him, and he gave her a quick kiss. Then, looking around the room, he asked, "Where's your bag?"

She pointed to it sitting beside the front door.

"Okay, then. Ready?" Tyler raised his eyebrows hopefully.

Robbie grabbed her short down jacket, locked the door behind her, and followed Tyler out to his waiting car. The early morning air was sharp and crisp, and a frost as thick as snow lay on the long-dead grass.

The realization that Tyler wanted to be with her this much gave Robbie a pleasant little glow. As he maneuvered the sportscar smoothly through the heavy morning traffic and concentrated on driving, she kept glancing over at his classic profile, thinking how lucky she was and feeling a thrill of anticipation at having nearly three whole days together with a man she was coming to adore.

Once out on the freeway heading north, Tyler opened the glove compartment and tossed a sheaf of brochures in her lap. "Take a look at these and you'll get an idea of what it's like up there," he instructed. "Most of that kind of literature is press agent hype, but Beech Mountain really is a skier's dream. I've been to both Squaw Valley in California and Aspen, and it's every bit as good," Tyler commented.

Robbie looked at the full-color, lavishly illustrated folders promising all kinds of delights for both the adventurous skier and the fireside sitter and shopper. "It looks great!" she had to agree.

The farther they drove and the nearer they got, the more she found herself looking forward to the weekend. Most of all, she wanted to match Tyler's own obvious enthusiasm. The fact that he had planned it all as a surprise for her gave her new hope that their relationship was becoming even more important to him. As an experienced ski enthusiast he could have chosen another solo weekend of uncomplicated skiing. Instead, he was dragging along a neophyte who might hamper his own pleasure in the sport. Robbie looked over at him, feeling suddenly shy. *Why else would Ty have arranged this weekend if he hadn't wanted to spend some special time exclusively with me?*

What was it he had said? "I want you to enjoy the things I enjoy. I want us to do things together. I didn't want to go away on another ski trip without you!"

They stopped for lunch. The attractive rustic restaurant was filled with other people whose garb and conversation clearly indicated they, too, were bound for a weekend in the snow.

"This place specializes in fantastic hamburgers," Tyler mentioned as they were handed huge hand-printed menus. "And if you have any room left after one of them, they serve a fabulous apple pie with hot cinnamon sauce!"

"Stop!" Robbie held her hand up in laughing protest. "If I eat like this all weekend I'll be suspended from flying for being overweight!"

"Come on!" Tyler scoffed. "*You?*"

The waitress came for their order, and Robbie gave an exaggerated sigh and said, "Well, I'll have one of the jumbo burgers with the works!"

"Good!" Tyler laughed and nodded in approval. "We'll probably have the pie, too." Then he added, "A la mode!"

After lunch they started on the second leg of their trip. The terrain was visibly changing, Robbie noticed. They were climbing now into mountainous areas, and here and there among the towering pines were patches of snow.

"The predictions for ski conditions are great this weekend," Tyler told her. With each passing mile Robbie could see his eagerness mounting.

"You have it too, I see," she commented after a while. "Yes, I believe it's a classic case—one of the most severe I've ever observed." She affected a crisp, professional tone of voice.

He turned and looked at her quizzically. "I don't get it. What are you talking about?"

"Didn't you hear that charter bus driver rounding up his passengers as we were leaving the restaurant?" she asked him.

"I guess not. Why?"

"He called, 'All patients with ski fever, line up for Beech Mountain bus. Guaranteed cure.'"

Tyler chuckled but added, "He's wrong, you know. It's only a temporary cure. Next weekend you come down with the same symptoms all over again!"

"Is it contagious?" quipped Robbie.

Tyler reached over and pressed her hand. "I hope so," he beamed.

Two hours later, after driving along a spectacular stretch of road through snow-covered hills dotted with dark green pines, they arrived at Beech Mountain. As Tyler parked the car, Robbie saw that they were in a setting that easily could have been Gstaad in the Swiss Alps. People in bright ski clothes milled along the streets as a holiday atmosphere electrified the air. Skiers could be seen on the hills surrounding the little town. They looked like tiny toy figures moving down the slopes.

The lodge was a large, low-roofed building of native stone and timber. The lobby was crammed with people in a party mood. Loud greetings, talk, and laughter filled the huge room with sound.

Tyler, holding Robbie firmly by the arm, elbowed his way to the desk through the clusters of gaily dressed guests. "There may still be a chance to get on the slopes this afternoon," Tyler said expectantly.

After they had registered at the desk, Tyler was directed to check with the ski information booth. Robbie urged him, "You go ahead, Ty. I'll freshen up and meet you after you have had your run. I'm sure there are no beginner groups this late in the day."

He hesitated a split second and then agreed. "You're sure you don't mind? If I can catch a lift, I can get one good downhill—" His eyes snapped with excitement.

Robbie watched Ty disappear as the clusters of chatting vacationers parted to let him through and then closed again into tight circles. Her room key in hand, she made her way to the elevator and stepped into the crowded enclosure. The ski talk that swirled around her might as well have been partially in another language! She gathered from all she overheard that the snowpack this week was "terrific" and the skiing so far had been "fantastic"—good news for Ty for sure. But for herself? The little nagging worry about coming began to tighten her stomach again.

What if this were some kind of test? Maybe Tyler wanted to see how she functioned in a totally unfamiliar setting, but that seemed unlikely. After all, plenty of girls he knew who *did* ski would have jumped at an invitation like this.

He wants to be with you! Didn't he say so? Stop being so insecure, Robbie encouraged herself. *Okay! Okay!* she retorted. *All I can do is be myself.*

Her room was rustic, but luxurious, Robbie noted as she stepped into the deep shag-carpeted room and looked around. Tyler had made the reservations, and these had to be expensive accommodations. Robbie frowned. This whole trip had come up so unexpectedly he had not given her much time to think about the protocol of it. Should she have allowed him to pay for her room? It would be awkward now for her even to broach the subject, but she did feel a little strange about it. Of course, he could afford it, but still. . . .

Robbie shooed away the uneasiness she felt. It was too late to start fretting about whether she should have come or not. She was here now, so she was not going to say or do anything to make Tyler uncomfortable or to put herself in an embarrassing position. She would simply assume that their situation was the same as it had been in Bermuda or when they were seeing each other in Atlanta.

The adjoining bathroom was luxuriously appointed as well, complete with gold-flecked brown tile, thick beige and brown towels, and a step-in shower with several shower heads on the side walls. Robbie took a long, hot shower and then looked over her hastily packed weekend wardrobe. Pants or a long skirt for dinner? She had seen pictures of aprés-ski outfits in fashion magazines, but she was not sure whether this lodge was formal or casual. *Better casual tonight,* she reasoned, *and then see what the general trend is for tomorrow. Saturday night is probably the big dress-up night, anyway.* She put on royal blue corduroy pants and a lighter blue velour top with a stand-up collar that framed her face becomingly.

Robbie went over to the window and looked out. Through the frosty pane she saw that it was already dark. A cobalt blue sky hung as a backdrop to the various buildings with lighted windows that were orange squares casting rainbow-colored patterns on the white snow. On the hillside, little flickers of lights marked the trails for the late skiers' return. It was the proverbial winter wonderland.

The phone rang, and Robbie hurried to answer it. A second later she heard Tyler say, "I just got down a little while ago. Meet me in the lounge in fifteen minutes? I'm starved, aren't you?"

"Don't you think of anything but food?" she teased.

There was the slightest pause before he said, "Yes . . . but I'm trying to sublimate."

Robbie was glad he could not see her blush. "I'll see you in a few minutes," she said softly.

As she stepped off the elevator, Robbie was the object of several admiring glances. Everything about her glowed. The russet sheen of her casually brushed hair, the look of shining expectancy in her eyes, and the intriguing dimples at the corners of her upturned mouth all gave her a look of vibrance. She glanced around, looking for Tyler, unaware that any number of unattached males would have willingly approached her.

Suddenly she spotted him. Although he was facing the elevator, he had been distracted momentarily in conversation—and his strong, handsome head was bent toward a slender blonde in a purple jumpsuit and a young man.

Robbie hesitated to join them. But just then, as if somehow alerted, Tyler turned and his eyes met hers. Immediately Robbie felt that sharp throb under her heart that only he could cause, and she caught her breath.

Tyler's tanned face had deepened to a ruddy bronze from his afternoon on the slopes. His golden ochre hair, usually carefully groomed in town, was tousled and wind-blown, giving him a carefree, unstudied air. Wearing a natural-colored Irish fisherman's sweater and standing beside the glowing fireplace, he might have posed for one of the lodge's publicity advertisements.

As soon as he saw Robbie, he raised the glass he was holding in a toasting gesture. She saw his lips moving as he said something to his companions. The gorgeous blonde turned and gave Robbie a slow inventory with cool, appraising eyes. Tyler detached himself from the group and started across the crowded room toward Robbie.

Tyler's arm circled her waist, and he asked, "What took you so long?" He bent his lips to her ear and whispered, "I missed you." He brushed her check with a kiss and told her, "Come on, I want some people to meet you."

Robbie thought happily, *He said to meet you, not the other way around.*

They ate dinner with a crowd seated at a round table in the dining room that fairly hummed with laughing voices, above the sound of clinking glasses and bursts of song. Skiers, Robbie was discovering, were a fun-loving bunch, and the room rang with a feeling of good fellowship. Although Tyler joined in actively in the table talk that was largely a discussion of the day's skiing and tomorrow's weather, he was very attentive to Robbie. He heaped her plate with generous amounts of salad and urged her to try the three different kinds of fondue in the center of the table.

Even though she could not participate much in the ski talk, Robbie nevertheless began to feel perfectly at ease and comfortable. As they all lingered over coffee after dinner, Ty's arm was draped casually over the back of her chair, establishing them definitely as a couple. It gave Robbie a warm feeling.

When he leaned down and whispered, "Let's get out of here. Take a walk? I want you all to myself for a while," Robbie's reaction was a foolish kind of gladness.

"I'll get my jacket," she whispered back.

She found herself heading for the elevator at the same time as Regina Overstreet, the blonde she had first noticed standing with Tyler when she had come down to meet him earlier. Again Robbie felt herself the target of a sweeping appraisal. When she met Regina's steady gaze, Robbie saw the blonde's eyes widen slightly, but then she asked ingenuously, "Are you and Ty an item?"

A little taken aback, Robbie hesitated.

"I mean is he your boyfriend?" When Robbie did not answer right away, Regina persisted, "The reason I'm asking is because he comes up here all the time to ski, but this is the first time he's ever brought anyone. We were all just wondering . . ." She let her sentence trail off insinuatingly.

Suddenly the elevator doors slid open and, in the crush of people getting off as well as going in, Robbie was rescued from giving an answer—an answer she really didn't have.

Did Tyler consider her his girlfriend? *Were* they an item? It was interesting to learn that he had never brought any other girl up here with him before.

Robbie darted to a corner of the crowded elevator and wedged a burly man between herself and Regina. After a glance at Robbie, the blonde began talking to someone else.

Outside, the air was so clear and cold that it almost took Robbie's breath away. As she greeted Tyler, who was waiting near the door, clouds of frosty smoke spun from her mouth. He took her hand and tucked it with his into one of the fleece-lined pockets of his suede coat. The sky, now a deep velvety purple, rose around them like a canopy held up by the shimmering snow-capped hills. The frozen crust of snow crunched crisply under their booted footsteps as they walked hand in hand down to the skating rink in the silver light of a half-dollar moon.

"Having fun?" Tyler asked Robbie.

She looked up at him and nodded.

"Tomorrow will be even better. I'm going to introduce you to one of life's greatest pleasures," he promised.

"Oh? What's that?" Robbie took the bait.

"Skiing, naturally. I've already talked to Detmar. He's one of the instructors—very good, very patient, the best. He'll have you started before you know it, and the right

125

way. You won't have to unlearn any bad habits like I did." He paused and then added jokingly, "He is also extremely handsome and quite a ladies' man. I'm just warning you."

"Don't bother. I'm not the least bit susceptible, I promise you," Robbie replied.

"How come you're so sure?" Ty persisted.

"A ski instructor? Me?" she laughed. "I have a confession to make. I'm pretty uncoordinated. In school I was always the last one chosen when they were picking teams."

They had reached the open-air skating rink, and they leaned on the encircling rail and looked at the still, glistening expanse of ice. Tyler's arm went around Robbie, drawing her close. She felt the buttery smoothness of suede under her cheek as she leaned against him. The crystal night was exquisitely still. Far in the distance they could hear the slightest echo of disco music from the lodge's dance floor, and the faint sound of voices and laughter wafted through the clear, cold air. But the only thing Robbie was truly conscious of was T. J.

It was he who broke the quiet, as he gave her a quick, hard hug. "Let's go. It's been a long day, and you have to be up to report for your skiing lesson at eight sharp!"

Robbie stifled a little moan.

"I'm telling you you're going to love it," Tyler said gently just before he kissed her. His lips were warm, soft, searching. Robbie was swept up into the magic of the night. Her arms wound around Tyler's neck, as she responded to the deep stirring throb of feeling within her. She could feel his hands pressing her closer, and she let herself surrender to the enchantment of the moment. Slowly he released her, and the spinning space gradually slowed to the real world. Robbie's happiness made her slightly dizzy, and she laughed with the joy of it.

"Come on, I'll take you in," Tyler said huskily.

They walked back to the lodge with their arms around each other. Just before they reached the steps, Tyler halted and drew her back into the shadows and kissed her again.

From somewhere down in the valley came the sound of sleigh bells, and they broke apart smiling. "Did you hear bells?" Tyler asked. Robbie nodded. At that moment, a group of laughing celebrators came bursting out into the night, noisily passing by them.

Back in her room minutes later, Robbie dreamily pushed open the bedroom window and leaned out. The pine-studded hills, the lights shining out on the snowy banks, and the quaint shapes of the different houses and condos along the winding village streets made the scene below look like a giant Christmas card. The whole place had a fairy-tale setting, and Robbie wasn't sure that she might not wake up the next morning and find it had all been a dream.

Robbie raised her eyes to the dark velvet sky, twinkling with a myriad of stars. *Oh, Lord, the beauty and the joy of this time are so fantastic. Help me to find what is real and right for my life.*

The next morning a banner of sunlight flooded her room with dazzling light. Outside, sunshine sparkled on the snow in a thousand diamond lights. After breakfast Tyler escorted her to the site where the snow bunny class was forming, gave her an encouraging pat on the shoulder, and left to catch an early chairlift ride to one of the steepest slopes, promising to meet her at lunch.

"Well, how did it go?" Tyler asked eagerly when Robbie, rosy-cheeked and aching from the unaccustomed use of several newly discovered muscles in her arms, shoulders, and legs, met him on the lodge's upper sundeck for lunch.

"Why don't you ask Detmar?" Robbie fielded his question as she lowered herself gingerly into the chair opposite him at their corner table.

"As a matter of fact, I ran into him just now, and he said you were terrific! Had real potential!"

"Hah!" was Robbie's derisive comment.

"Come on, seriously . . ." Tyler probed.

Robbie eyed him speculatively. He had on dark glasses, so it was hard to tell if he were teasing or really interested in her morning's progress.

"Well, since my class consisted of two ten-year-old boys, a seven-year-old girl, and a nun, I held my own!" she exclaimed facetiously and dissolved into helpless laughter. "You really should have been there! Once I fell down and was laughing so hard I couldn't get up. Even Detmar—who incidentally takes his instruction chores very seriously—finally had to give in and laugh, too. But it *was* fun . . . and I imagine after about a hundred lessons I might be able to keep my legs together long enough to make it down a small hill!"

A statuesque girl with a golden braid to her waist and attired in fitted black ski pants and a red sweater brought their lunch.

"I ordered for you," Tyler explained. "After noon there'll be a real crush here for lunch, and I wanted to get back for an afternoon's skiing."

The waitress put a luscious, large submarine sandwich and a steaming mug of fragrant coffee in front of Robbie, who realized she was famished. When the girl left, Robbie leaned across the table and in a stage whisper asked, "Is every female around here blonde and beautiful? I'm beginning to think it's some kind of conspiracy against the rest of us."

"You don't have anything to worry about, believe me!" Tyler said solemnly. "In the sun, your hair's like a newly minted penny, and your skin looks like an Ivory Soap commercial. This mountain air is a great enhancer of beauty," he told her.

"Did you sign up for another lesson this afternoon?" Tyler asked her.

Robbie shook her head. "No, I don't want too much of a good thing!" She rolled her eyes comically.

"Well, what will you do? I don't like leaving you alone."

"Tyler, did you get a look at all the shops?" she demanded. "I can certainly find plenty to do. Don't give it another thought. I'll find lots to do and have fun besides," she reassured him.

The afternoon sped by just as Robbie had promised Tyler. In fact, she was surprised when she glanced at her watch and saw that it was nearly five. She had browsed happily all afternoon in the various gift shops, clothing stores, and boutiques. When she greeted Tyler in the lounge at five-thirty, she was wearing one of her new purchases, a light blue Alpine sweater with a yoke of brilliant embroidery, worn with a long skirt.

Tyler brought their mocha espressos topped with a swirl of nutmeg-sprinkled whipped cream over to the cushioned circle surrounding the pit fireplace in the lounge. He handed Robbie a cup and then seated himself beside her. "Have fun shopping?" he asked.

She took a sip of the delicious hot drink and nodded.

"I did a little shopping myself." Tyler grinned. "I got done a little earlier than I planned, and I saw something I thought you might like, a small reminder of the weekend." He reached behind him and held out a small square box. "It's for you."

Robbie lifted the top off the box, pushed the tissue paper aside, and took out a Tyrolean wooden music box. The two tiny carved gaily painted little figures on top were on skis. "Oh, Ty, it's darling!" she exclaimed. "Thank you."

"Here, listen," he said and tipped it slightly to wind the key underneath. The sweet, tinkling melody was "Edelweiss," from one of Robbie's all-time favorite musicals, *The Sound of Music.*

"Every time you hear it, I'll hope you'll think of this time and of *us.*" He spoke quietly, his eyes very intense.

"I will," Robbie replied and leaned over to kiss him lightly. Just then some people who knew T. J. came into the lounge and hailed him. They all ended up having dinner together, and it was not until much later that Robbie and T. J. were alone again.

"Our last night here," Tyler said when the three other couples had left the table to dance. "We should do something special. I certainly don't want to spend it yakking about skiing with a dozen people." He frowned.

"Let's walk down to the skating rink again," she said softly.

"Let's," he said, taking her hand and pulling her to her feet.

Robbie shivered as they left the warmth of the lounge. Immediately Tyler put his arm around her and drew her close.

"This has been a—" he halted. "I can't even think of the right word for it—*some* weekend," he finished lamely. "Have you enjoyed it?" he asked Robbie.

"Yes! I even think I could develop ski fever," she laughed. "Seriously, Ty, I've loved it. Thank you for bringing me."

He stopped, turning her in his embrace.

"Thank you for coming!" he said gently and kissed her, a long, infinitely sweet kiss.

Back in Atlanta on Sunday night, Robbie placed the little music box on her dressing table, touching it tenderly as the precious symbol of the most fabulous weekend she had ever spent. She twisted the tiny key, and the familiar lilting melody flooded her memory with the magic of their last hour together on the night before they left. The lounge had been almost empty when they had returned from the skating rink. Most of the skiers, anxious to get their rest before the last ski morning of the weekend, had deserted the lobby. Only the piano player and a few other couples had been lingering there when Robbie and Tyler had entered. Tyler had brought them hot spiced cider from the bar and had stopped at the piano before joining Robbie in front of the fire. When the notes of "Edelweiss" had begun to play softly, Robbie knew Tyler must have requested it.

Everything—the firelight, the whisper of the snow that had begun to fall against the windows, the mellow music in the background, the feelings of closeness and intimacy—had combined to make Robbie admit to herself that she had lost her heart. *But not my head*, she had reminded herself—at least, not yet. She had to be sure, really sure, that T. J. was the one whom the Lord had planned for her. Until then . . .

She wound the little key again and sang along with the haunting melody, "Edelweiss, edelweiss, every morning you greet me." She had read somewhere that the edelweiss was a tiny blue flower found in the highest crevices of the Austrian Alps—and was the symbol of enduring love.

Did T. J. know the meaning of the words of the song played by the music box he had given her? Or was it simply that the pretty little box with its figures on skis seemed an appropriate gift for a ski weekend?

She couldn't be sure. All she could do was hope and dream—and *pray!*

Chapter Fourteen

After that weekend at Beech Mountain, Robbie Mallory was certain that she was in love with Tyler J. Lang. None of the things she had warned herself about before seemed to matter now. With the blind optimism of someone completely in love, she told herself that everything would fall into place eventually. Their personalities, viewpoints, and lifestyles, different as they might seem, would merge, blend, and become one gradually. In time everything would work out.

When she was not with him, she longed to be. In between their respective flight schedules, they spent as much time together as they could manage.

Dazed as she was by the wonder of it, sometimes, without wanting it, doubts nibbled at her happiness. When she thought of Tyler's kisses and the embraces that had thrilled her and brought her to the awareness of desire, she felt a delight that was both provocative and frightening. When she remembered how she had felt that night at his apartment, in his arms, she remembered with a cold, shuddering clarity how close she had come to complete surrender.

I have to be careful, she warned herself. *I might be deluded into doing something foolish by my own feelings. With all he has to offer, I could be misled to think it is enough. And I know it's not. Until he's ready to make that ultimate commitment I cannot let myself be overwhelmed.*

I'm sure he loves me, Robbie told herself over and over. *I'll just have to be patient. When he's ready, he'll tell me,* she assured herself. *Until then, I'm just going to be happy!*

On a cold, windy afternoon in the second week in February, Robbie was just in from a flight and coming up the steps to her apartment. As she put her key in the lock, she could hear the shrill sound of the phone ringing. Tossing her handbag and gloves on the couch and not bothering to take off her coat, she ran to answer it.

"Have you got some coffee made?" asked the voice that never failed to thrill her.

"I just got in," she answered breathlessly as she tucked the receiver under her chin and shrugged out of her coat.

"How about putting a pot on? I'm coming over," Tyler said bruskly.

"Yes, sir!" she laughed.

She hurried to her small kitchen, filled the kettle, and put it on the stove to boil.

Cyrano, who had been huddled by the door when Robbie had come up on the deck, had slipped in when she opened the door and now wound himself around her ankles, meowing loudly. "Okay, okay!" Robbie laughed. "You male creatures are all impatient!"

After she had put the filter in the coffeepot and measured in the coffee, she got out the carton of half-and-half, filled the cream pitcher, and then poured a generous amount into a saucer and set it on the floor for Cyrano.

By now Robbie knew that it took Ty a little less than forty minutes, barring unusually heavy traffic, to come across town to her apartment. She had time for a quick shower and change.

The kettle shrilled, and she poured boiling water into the top of the glass pot and breathed in the rich aroma as the dark liquid began to seep through.

In the shower, Robbie remembered that it was only two days until Valentine's Day and that she had bought Tyler two cards. One was humorous and the other lacy, beflowered, and sentimental. Was it too early to give them to him today—or maybe just one? Or would it look as if she were hinting for him to give her something? She didn't know. She'd wait, play it by ear, see how the evening went.

She was sure that Tyler must have checked her schedule and wanted to take her out for something to eat and then to a movie. There was one about spies playing at a theater nearby which they had talked about seeing. Maybe when they came back after the movie she'd give the cards to him.

In and out in ten minutes, she fluffed her hair and put on gray slacks, a tailored gray silk blouse, and a yellow cardigan. Eyeing the music box on her dressing table, Robbie opened the small leather jewel box next to it, took out the coral beads, and clasped them around her neck. Her hand touched them briefly. Funny, how these simple gifts of Tyler's meant so much to her, and she knew he liked to see her wearing the Bermudian beads.

Back in the kitchen she got out the mugs, which they had bought one day in a pottery shop, and sugar and was setting them on the counter between the kitchen and the living room when she heard his footsteps on the stairs, followed a minute later by his familiar knock.

Immediately Tyler opened the door and walked in. Robbie's heart gave a small leap as it always did when she saw him. He was wearing an oatmeal cable-knit sweater, brown corduroy pants, and desert boots.

"Hi, there!" she called from behind the counter, her eyes bright with happiness. "Your order's ready, sir!"

He crossed the room and straddled one of the high stools on the other side. Robbie started to lean over for a kiss, but something in Tyler's expression stopped her. Instead, she filled their mugs with coffee.

"Want something else? I have some brownies—courtesy of Sara Lee," she said, attempting humor. Something about Tyler's demeanor puzzled her. He looked depressed.

"No thanks, just coffee." He put in a spoonful of sugar, added cream, and stirred it a couple of times. "I just want to talk. I mean, I came over because I have something I need to tell you."

The impersonal tone of his voice bothered her. An icy ripple like a cold finger drizzled down her spine. What was this all about? What did Tyler have to tell her?

"I want you to know this isn't some sudden impulse. It's something I've been thinking about for quite a while." He stirred his coffee a little longer and then said, "I think we should stop seeing each other."

The shock was like a physical blow. Robbie's throat contracted, and she tried to swallow around its tightness. His words had sounded very loud in the suddenly quiet room.

Robbie's heart began to bang crazily, and her ears roared. Her first reaction was, *He's met someone else. It has happened, just like people said it would. His romances never last.*

She listened in stunned silence as Tyler went on. "I'm going to level with you, Robbie. I think you're marvelous, very sweet, very special, but, I get the impression that you're the kind of girl who is looking for a storybook romance, one that ends in a chapel with orange blossoms, rice, and forever after in a rose-covered cottage. To put it bluntly, I'm not used to playing a waiting game. Very frankly, you should know I'm not the marrying kind. I'm thirty-three and I like being single. I don't want you to be hurt, because I do care about you. So, I think the best thing I could do for you is to back off now before we get any further involved."

He paused significantly, looking at her with a clear, steady gaze, as if giving the announcement time to sink in. His expression was noncommittal, his eyes shuttered, so she could not read what he might be thinking.

She caught her trembling lower lip with her teeth. She mustn't let him see how hurt she was or how near tears. "I think you're right," she told him in a soft, emotionless voice.

He cleared his throat and continued, "Before we met I'd been thinking about putting in for a transfer. Some place where I could do more sailing, with better weather year 'round to do the kind of things I enjoy. I took a couple of flights out to California so I could look around. Well, I've just been informed that there's an opening out there, and I'm going to take it. San Francisco."

"Oh? I see," was all she could muster.

Tyler stirred his coffee again. "Well, I guess I've said what I came to say. I hope you understand that it's all for the best." He got to his feet and walked to the door.

"When are you leaving?" she asked weakly.

"The fourteenth, day after tomorrow," he replied.

She had the crazy urge to laugh hysterically! Valentine's Day! What a day for a romance to end, to come to a crashing finish! But she managed to smile and say steadily, "Well, good luck, Tyler. I'm sure you'll like California."

"Good-bye, Robbie. All the best, okay?" He had his hand on the doorknob, but he still stood there.

Why didn't he leave, get out, go—so that she could fall apart in private?

"It's best all around, Robbie. You'll see." Tyler's voice was hoarse.

She nodded, silently screaming, *Please go!*

He yanked open the door, and a blast of cold wind chilled the room. Robbie shivered. The door shut loudly behind Tyler. She held herself rigid, listening to his footsteps on the wooden stairway and then the sound of the car's engine starting.

It was only then that she noticed her legs were trembling. She collapsed on the kitchen stool and put her head in both hands.

"It's for the best, Robbie," Tyler's words repeated themselves. It *must* be for the best. Then why did she feel so bereft?

It *was* for the best. She had to believe that. If they had been right for each other, wouldn't it have worked out? Wouldn't their differences have been resolved? Maybe, if she had not been so obvious and hadn't come on so strongly about her beliefs. No, it was self-defeating even to think like that, Robbie told herself sternly. If he couldn't accept her the way she was, her whole self, then . . . There was no use going over and over this.

The ironic thing was that Tyler had pinpointed all the things she had told herself. Strange, that he should be the one to break up their relationship. In a way she resented it, because he had robbed her of her right to be righteous, nobly giving *him* up!

She shook her head at her own weakness. It was she who had been the fool. Tyler was perceptive enough to see that they were too different to bridge the chasm between them. He probably had met someone without her "outdated morals," her "hang-ups," or, as he teased, her "Victorian viewpoint" on life.

Well, she was well out of it! Robbie told herself firmly. It had not gone too far. She would get over it.

It was not until later that evening, when she was unpacking her suitcase and found the two valentines intended for Tyler, that Robbie began to cry.

Chapter Fifteen

March was bitterly cold. On the Chicago-Denver route Robbie's flights often were plagued with rain, fog, sleet, head winds, and blizzard conditions. The weather seemed to reflect her own inner storms. Depression wrapped itself around her, smothering her spirits. The heady, unreal excitement of her brief romance with Tyler haunted her.

The abrupt ending was what stung. But would it have been any easier if she had followed her first inclinations and broken it off herself? *At least my pride wouldn't be so damaged.* But, to tell the truth, she had been dazzled by Tyler, flattered by his attention, and had fallen in love with a lack of caution that was uncharacteristic. After all, she had been forewarned about him but had ignored the caveats and rushed headlong into the romance. Actually, she had no one to blame but herself.

Coming off flight one blustery March afternoon, Robbie felt unusually tired. It had been a rough trip. They had been delayed all along the route, held for weather, then, because of other flights with time priority, held for both takeoffs and landings. By the time they finally had made it to Atlanta, they were four hours late. She was looking forward to nothing more than hurrying home, kicking off her high heels, and luxuriating in a long, relaxing bubble bath.

However, after she had filed her flight log in Operations, she stopped by the stewardess lounge to check her mailbox and found an intercompany envelope from the Chief Stewardess's office. Inside was a memo.

> To: Roblynn Mallory
> From: Kara Collins, Chief Stewardess
> Please stop by my office when you return from Chicago. *Important.*

Robbie groaned inwardly—another delay. Well, she might as well get it over with, whatever it was, so she could enjoy her three days off.

The Chief Stewardess's office was on executive row in the administration building and very plush. The walls were the familiar Trans-Continent blue, the thick carpets the deeper blue of the uniform's trim. The furnishings were luxurious—pale blue leather sofas and chairs as comfortable as the lounge seats in First Class jets. Behind the secretary's desk was a huge mural of a cerulean blue sky with a Trans-Con super jet soaring into the clouds.

Kara's secretary was a pretty blonde who, when Robbie gave her name, picked up a blue phone, pressed one of a number of buttons on another blue instrument, and announced in a low, cultivated voice, "Miss Mallory to see you, Miss Collins."

Almost immediately, the door beyond the secretary's desk opened, and Kara, model-slim and exquisitely groomed, stepped out, smiled, and beckoned Robbie into her private office.

"Good flight?" Kara asked as she motioned Robbie to a chair opposite her curved pale fruitwood desk.

"The worst!" Robbie replied. Kara laughed knowingly as she seated herself and began looking through a folder on her desk. Robbie sat down in the comfortable armchair, eased her feet out of her pumps, and wiggled her toes in the deep shag.

Feeling frazzled and less than perfectly groomed, Robbie observed the Chief Stewardess with awe. With every sculptured dark wave in place and the blue bow-necked blouse complimenting her lovely skin and violet eyes, Kara Collins was the epitome of a glamorous career woman. She had been a flight attendant for years before taking this job, which negated the myth that the rapid turnover among Trans-Continent stewardesses was due to the fact that they all married wealthy passengers whom they had met on flight. Some of the stewardesses went on to top executive jobs in the company.

"First, I want to congratulate you, Robbie," Kara said with a dazzling smile. "You've just completed your one million miles flying with Trans-Continent! Here's your pin." She leaned across the desk and presented Robbie with a small box. Inside was a pin in the form of a pair of gold wings flanking a tiny blue globe on which was etched the outline of the United States. Underneath in gold was "1,000,000 miles."

"Wow!" Robbie said in a low voice. "I didn't realize—"

"You've done a terrific job for TCA," Kara beamed. "I've never received a single complaint about you, Robbie—not from any member of the crew you've flown with or any passenger you had on flight! In fact, we've had some very complimentary reports about you!"

"That's nice to hear," murmured Robbie.

"That's one of the reasons I called you in today. We have a proposal that we hope you will seriously consider. We would like you to represent TCA in a promotional tour this spring. It will cover twelve cities in six states—all new routes that TCA is opening up. It will involve your appearing on TV, attending civic luncheons, dinners, giving a short talk about TCA and what it's like to be a stewardess. You may be asked to go to high school career days in some cases, all very informal—things I know you won't find difficult to do. We think you'll be a great public relations plus for TCA. So, what about it? We'll put you on special leave, and you'll continue to get your same base pay plus flying pay as on your regular schedule, and of course all your travel expenses. How does that sound?"

"Sort of overwhelming!" Robbie exclaimed. "How long will it take?"

"Probably about a month, six weeks at the most. We want to see how it goes. It may turn out to be such a good thing for TCA that our public relations department may want to extend it, adding a few more cities in some of the states we already service. But, as of now, I'd say six weeks."

"May I think it over?" Robbie asked.

"Oh, surely. But you will let us know as soon as possible? Our advertising department wants to get to work on the advance publicity."

As she drove home along the freeway, Robbie kept reviewing the conversation with Kara. What an unexpected thing to happen just now. Ever since her breakup with Tyler, Robbie had been fighting a sense of purposelessness in her life and her job. In fact, this very day, when she had come off the plane and walked through the terminal, she had been thinking, *Another flight, another log to file, another four thousand miles flown.* Another day of her life had flown by. And where had she gone? She'd simply turned around and flown back the same distance—nothing gained. It had just added to the one million miles she had already flown. Robbie gave a mirthless little laugh. *I've flown a million miles and gotten nowhere.*

She pulled into the driveway and braked the car. Leaning on the steering wheel, she looked at the small patch of garden where she had planted bulbs. A few brave yellow daffodils nodded their bonneted heads in the cold wind. Something touched Robbie with melancholy. Since losing Tyler, the whole world had become a heavy, joyless thing.

The gray winter day made her think longingly of the pastel-colored houses, soft sea breeze, and shell-pink beach of Bermuda.

She thought of that first meeting. How often she had tried to forget it, but it kept coming back to her. It had been the beginning of the happiest period of her life—a beginning that had ended like an unfinished melody. That was what was so troubling. It remained there always, dangling tantalizingly, hauntingly incomplete. But could it have ended any other way?

Bittersweet memories are the worst. There is always that possibility that somehow you might have worked things out, that somehow it had not needed to end the way it had.

I have got to stop thinking this way! And about him! Robbie told herself.

She got out of the car, dragged her suitcase from the back, and started wearily up the outside steps to the apartment. Halfway up, she thought she heard her phone ringing and began to run. Her hand shook as she tried to get the key into the lock and open the door. By the time she rushed inside, the phone was mockingly silent. Maybe it had not even rung at all.

Robbie shook her head as if to clear it. She had gotten into the stupid habit of expecting the phone to ring. Waiting for it to ring was a habit that would be hard to break, but she would have to break it if she ever were going to get on with her life. She could not live on memories.

Maybe the thing to do was to accept the offer for the promotional tour Kara had presented. Maybe that was the change she needed.

Exhausted, she did not even bother to fix herself something to eat. Instead, she merely undressed and fell into bed. Although her body cried out for sleep and rest, her mind raced. Finally she prayed, *Lord, forgive me. I asked for guidance and then didn't follow it. I asked You to show me the way, and I wasn't brave enough to take it. So, now, I'm coming to You, again. This time I promise to obey. If this tour is what You want me to do, then I'll go.*

She had one more scheduled flight this month. When she got back from that, she would go see Kara Collins again. By that time she would know what to do.

Chapter Sixteen

When the plane landed in Denver, the air was crystal clear with the scent of snow and a brilliant blue sky. Sunlight reflected dazzlingly from the snow-capped mountains that rimmed the airport.

Robbie had had special responsibility for a ten-year-old girl, Sandi Spencer, on the trip all the way from Atlanta. It was Trans-Continent's policy that, when minors flew alone, they had to be in First Class under the supervision and care of stewardesses until they were met by an authorized person at their destination.

After most of the passengers had deplaned, Robbie took the little girl's hand and said, "Come on, Sandi, let's go find your daddy."

The huge airport lobby was swirling with currents of milling passengers, arriving or departing, along with people seeing them off or greeting them. Robbie moved through the throngs, intent on getting her charge to the Trans-Continent information booth, where they were to meet Sandi's father.

A sudden tug on her hand and the child's delighted cry of "Daddy! Daddy!" alerted Robbie to the happy fact that the tall man hurrying toward them was Sandi's father, Martin Spencer. He was appropriately grateful for the care Robbie had given his daughter.

Sandi looked up at Robbie, smiled shyly, and begged, "Walk out to the front with us, Robbie!"

Outside in the bitingly sharp wind, Robbie stood with them until Mr. Spencer's company car pulled up in front. The usual confusion and apparent chaos of major city airports prevailed. Rows of taxis, shuttle buses, and cars were lined up, with horns blowing impatiently, loading and unloading passengers. Piles of luggage, baggage carts, and rushing skycaps cluttered the apron of the terminal building. Over all resounded the roar of jets taking off and landing.

Robbie bid the little girl an affectionate good-bye as Sandi flung herself against her in a hug.

"You certainly must have made an impression," Martin Spencer observed with a grin.

"I want to be a stewardess when I grow up, Daddy. I want to be like Robbie."

The adults smiled over the little girl's head. With a final wave they pulled away, and Robbie turned to go back into the terminal. Suddenly she heard a deep, familiar voice call her name. She whirled around to see Tyler striding toward her! A Trans-Con crew van had just let out Tyler, his copilot, and three flight attendants at the terminal entrance.

Robbie stood frozen to the spot, unable to move or speak. Her heart wrenched painfully at the sight of his lean frame, handsome in his dark blue uniform, the deep tan of his face, and the sun shining on his dark gold hair as he took off his cap. "Robbie! Wait!" he called.

As he came toward her, Robbie quickly slipped on dark glasses, as if to protect her golden-hazel eyes from the glare, but more to conceal any vulnerability that he might see there. T. J.'s unexpected appearance had wrought havoc with all her well-rehearsed composure if ever she happened to run into him. She was still easily moved by looking directly at his knowing eyes, twinkling with some secret joke, and his mouth whose kisses had left her eager for more.

Then he was standing in front of her. Without hesitation, he pulled her to him, his arms hugging her tight, laughing a low, throaty chuckle, his cheek cold and smooth as he pressed it against her face. Robbie tried to hold herself rigid and resist the silly weakness which she felt at his nearness.

"What a stroke of luck!" he was saying. "I kept hoping for something like this to happen. Come on, let's go some place where we can talk."

Speechless and apparently helpless, Robbie allowed him to take her arm, steering her through the revolving glass doors and across the terminal lobby toward the escalator. On the second level, still holding her arm, he stood for a minute, then shrugged. "I guess the coffee shop's our only bet."

A few minutes later they were sitting together in a booth surrounded by the clatter of plates, rattle of cutlery, and swish of busy waitresses moving through the jammed restaurant with trays and coffee carafes. *Hardly the place one would choose for such a meeting,* Robbie thought, trying to still her inner quivering. She knew she was nervous. Seeing Tyler had unleashed a thousand tingling sensations she thought she had extinguished.

You're so weak! she told herself scornfully. *He only has to look at you and you melt—snap his fingers and you come running!*

"Two coffees," Tyler told the hovering waitress, and she disappeared. Then he turned back to Robbie. His look pierced her heart like a lance. There was a question in his eyes she did not want to answer, and she lowered her own, not meeting his scrutiny.

Then he spoke in a low, intense tone of voice. "Have you missed me half as much as I've missed you?"

The waitress returned with their coffee. Robbie asked brightly, for her benefit, "How is California?"

"Anything else?" the waitress asked.

Tyler shook his head impatiently. "No thanks."

She went away.

"California is gorgeous, but I'm miserable," Tyler said fiercely. "I've always despised 'Monday morning quarterbacking' and that's what I've been doing—frankly—about us." He paused and shook his head, smiling. "I was wrong to write us off. I know I hurt you and I'm sorry. I honestly felt—at the time—it was the best thing—for *both* of us. But it was crazy to think I could forget you so easily. I haven't been able to get you off my mind or out of my heart. Is it too late to apologize?"

She took a sip of coffee, but it was too hot and scalded her tongue. She put the cup back down quickly.

Robbie felt breathless. Conscious of his nearness, she was aware of the familiar woodsy scent, that fresh clean aura that clung to him. He put out his hand and touched her arm, and the feel of his fingers through the sleeve of her blouse was warm, sending little sparks streaking up her arm. She drew in her breath and moved away a little. All the torrent of emotions she had tried to suppress came rushing back. She should be immune and hardened to his charm by now, but instead she felt more vulnerable and full of self-doubt. Had she been wrong about him after all?

"I miss you all the time," Tyler went on. "Everything I see, I want to show *you*. Everything I do, I want to do with *you*. Anywhere I think about going, I want to take you along."

Robbie sat as though mesmerized. No words came, but her heart began to race crazily.

"You'd love California. There's so much beauty, so much to enjoy. The coast! I drove down to Big Sur last weekend. It was magnificent. But all I could think of was how much Robbie would enjoy it," Tyler went on.

"I want you to see my apartment. It's got a view of the Golden Gate Bridge and the bay. You wouldn't believe the sunsets! I wish you could watch them with me." His eyes snapped with excitement. She hadn't seen him this enthusiastic since their ski trip. "Robbie, you've got to come out, see for yourself. Look, it could be arranged. Why don't you check on who has the Chicago-coast run? Switch flights and plan to work a flight out to San Francisco. Pull whatever strings you can. Then you'd have three days off out there. As soon as you get it set, call me. Here." He took out a card, scribbled something down, and handed it to her. "That's my apartment phone number, but you can always get me through West Coast personnel office. I'll coordinate my schedule so I can be off the same days. I'll show you all over. All the things I've wanted you to share with me—Fisherman's Wharf, Golden Gate Park—you'll go wild over the flowers there—and the zoo, and the Japanese Tea Garden. Then we'd go to Chinatown, take the ferry to Marin. . . . Oh, come on, say you'll do it!"

Tyler leaned across the table and said earnestly, "We've got to give ourselves a break, Robbie. Make up for lost time. I'll take the blame for messing things up for us. But we can make a fresh start. Please, don't say no. Think it over. We can start all over. I was wrong

150

when I thought it would be easy to break up before I left. But it can be fixed. Honey, trust me."

"But—" she began.

"It will be simple to arrange. When you get to San Francisco, instead of going to the airport motel with the rest of the crew, take the limo into the city and catch a cab to my apartment. If I'm not there—but, if I know ahead of time I can probably—anyway—"

Just then, over the PA system came the message, "Captain T. J. Lang, please report to Flight Operations."

Tyler swore under his breath and glanced at his watch. "Got to go file my flight plan. Now listen, Robbie, there's no problem if you can't work a flight. Get a non-rev on your days off. Let me know. I'll meet your flight; then we'll have three whole days to get everything straightened out between us, okay?"

"Captain Lang, please report immediately to Flight Operations," the voice came again, this time more insistently.

Tyler grabbed Robbie's wrist. "Walk with me," he said, jerking his head toward the door leading into the lobby.

All around them was the activity of the impersonal restaurant as they weaved their way between tables. *What a place to try to decide something as important as this*, Robbie thought.

Still holding her, Tyler moved rapidly toward the bank of Trans-Con ticket counters. Once there, he spoke to one of the agents. "May we use your office for a minute?"

The agent nodded. "Sure thing, Captain Lang." He pointed to the door behind him. Tyler pulled Robbie around the end of the counter and opened the door marked Private, Employees Only.

Once inside, he closed the door, pressing the snap lock. Then he took her in his arms and held her close. Her head went back to look at him, and for a second before he kissed her she wanted to laugh for sheer joy. The kiss was tender, full of longing and the passionate sweetness she still remembered.

Reluctantly Tyler released her. "I've got to go," he said. Then he took her hand, turned it palm up, placed something small, metallic, and cold into it, and folded her fingers over it. "Whatever you can work out, whenever you can come, use this. If I'm not there, wait for me. Let's not make the same mistake again, Robbie. We've wasted too much time already." He pulled her to him again and kissed her with an intensity that left her breathless.

T. J. was being paged again when he and Robbie came back into the lobby. He gave her one long, last look. His eyes moving over her were saying all the things that the time and situation prevented him from saying. Then, making a small salute, he turned and walked away. Robbie stood watching his tall figure stride through the terminal, mount the escalator, and disappear into the crowd.

Minutes later, her own return flight to Chicago was called. The announcement jolted Robbie back to reality, and she became acutely conscious of what Tyler had placed in her hand. She stared down at her outstretched palm and saw the shiny metal key—*the key to Tyler's San Francisco apartment.* All sorts of possible meanings flashed through her mind. Was this Tyler's way of telling her that he was ready to make the ultimate commitment?

She didn't have time right then to consider all the probable reasons. She slipped the key into her uniform skirt pocket and started walking toward her departure gate. She would have to wait to consider all the choices that Tyler had dangled before her until her preliminary flight duties were accomplished and they had taken off.

With a soaring heart, Robbie walked out onto the concourse toward the jet, relishing the winter sunshine and noticing that not a single cloud marred the clear blue of the Denver sky. Soon the giant plane had risen smoothly above the circling mountains.

Luckily there was a movie to be shown on this leg of the flight. After she had finished the beverage service and made the rounds handing out earphones to those who wanted to watch, magazines to those who didn't, and pillows to passengers who wanted to sleep, Robbie took a seat in the back of the First Class section and reviewed the surprising encounter with Tyler.

She thought she understood now why Tyler had backed off so abruptly when their romance had begun to get serious. Robbie remembered his remarking once how many marriages among his fellow pilots had gone on the rocks. She had the impression then that Tyler was afraid of marriage. When he had realized he might be falling in love with her, he hadn't wanted to take a chance. But the message of his words today seemed different. Maybe now he was willing to risk it. If only she could show him that marriage was not a trap or a ticket to emotional disaster—convince him that marriage could be the most wonderful adventure in life for two people truly committed to each other and loving and growing together in an exclusive relationship.

An icy rain turning quickly into sleet was falling when they landed in Chicago. Robbie had an hour and a half before the flight resumed to Atlanta. She went up to the stewardess lounge to freshen up.

To think that Tyler had missed her so much sent funny little shivers of excitement all through her! It was almost as if he had fallen in love with her against his will, she thought smiling. She remembered how she had given up hope that he would ever call her after their time in Bermuda, and then he had. And how he had sheepishly told her about it on a later date.

"Actually I tried *not* to call you," he had said slowly. "I mean, it was a conscious decision. I thought it might not be a good idea to see you again." He had stopped, laughed, and shrugged his shoulders. "You see how good I am at following my own advice?"

Robbie smiled in retrospect. Beneath all that surface sophistication, Tyler was sometimes startlingly open. In spite of himself and in spite of moving three thousand miles away, today he had told her it wasn't working. The invincible Tyler Lang had succumbed like any other guy in love, Robbie thought with a melting sensation. A man like that was impossible not to love.

Just then, the door of the stewardess lounge pushed open and Robbie saw a slender, blonde Trans-Continent stewardess rush in. A minute later, Robbie recognized her and whirled around exclaiming, "Sue Thompson!"

The other girl shrieked in return, "Robbie Mallory!" Sue Thompson had been in Robbie's flight attendants training class but was based in Florida, and the girls had not seen each other in nearly three years. After a rapid-fire interchange they sat down on the couch and began chatting merrily, swapping bits of news and gossip about the other girls who had graduated and received their wings together.

"But what in the world are you doing in Chicago?" asked Robbie. "I thought you were flying to the Virgin

Islands and the Philippines. Aren't you still based in Miami?"

A mischievous twinkle sparkled in Sue's wide, baby-blue eyes. She gave a little toss of her dandelion fluff curls, wrinkled her small kittenish nose, and smiled. The enchanting dimples on either side of her rosy mouth deepened. "We-l-l-l!" she drew out the word with exaggerated reluctance. "It's a long story and—I'm not sure I—I mean, it's kind of a secret."

"Uh-oh, there's a man in the picture somewhere!" teased Robbie.

Sue had been given an undisputed ten rating by her classmates when they had been in training. Sue was as sweet and friendly as she was beautiful, but it had been a running joke that she had received more male phone calls than any other girl in the entire six-week session. On Take-Off Day, two separate bouquets of a dozen long-stemmed roses each and an orchid corsage were delivered to Sue! Sue Thompson just naturally drew men with no seeming effort.

Sue reached over and squeezed Robbie's hand. "You're right, and there *is*! But, I can't tell!" She suddenly looked down at Robbie's wristwatch. "Oh, my goodness, is that the correct time? I've got to dash. Do I look a wreck?" she asked, bouncing up and peering anxiously in the mirror.

"Sue, you couldn't look a wreck if you were washed up on a desert island after a hurricane!" declared Robbie, watching Sue adjust her uniform cap. "But you still haven't told me how you happen to be in Chicago."

"I switched flights with a stewardess who has the run to Los Angeles and San Francisco—for a special reason, Robbie." She turned around from the mirror. "I really am sorry, but I promised not to tell anyone. It might get someone into trouble. Not bad trouble; it's just that it might be misinterpreted. . . ." She paused. "Gee, I've got to go, Robbie. It was super seeing you."

Sue went to the door. With her hand on its handle, she looked at Robbie, dimpled prettily, and said, "It's not that I don't think you're absolutely trustworthy, Robbie. In fact, I always said you were one of the nicest girls in our whole class—not mean or catty or anything. And I'd *like* to tell you what I'm going to be doing in San Francisco, but . . ." She sighed, put her hand in the outside pocket of her carry-on, and pulled something out. "You've heard of T. J. Lang, haven't you?" She held up a key and dangled it playfully. "Well, you can believe everything you've heard. He's the greatest!" She gave Robbie a wink and then waltzed out of the lounge, leaving Robbie stunned and gaping.

The full impact of what Sue had implied did not hit Robbie until a few seconds after Sue's jubilant exit.

Floods of emotion washed over her. She could feel the heat spread all through her as the humiliating facts began to take shape in her mind. Her breath came fast and shallow, as if she had been running a marathon. She felt sick and dizzy with the conflicting feelings of disbelief and anger.

Sue Thompson could have had no idea of Robbie's involvement with Tyler. Sue was too kind to try to hurt someone deliberately. Until this very minute, Robbie had had no idea that Tyler was seeing anyone else! She put clammy hands up to her suddenly throbbing temples! *How could he? After all he had just said?*

Bitterness came to her then like a hot, devouring flame. Tyler Lang was running true to form. How could she have ever thought he'd changed, that he was different because of her? His reputation had preceded him.

156

And she had known it when, against her better judgment, she had let herself fall in love with him.

She wanted to scream, sob, and pound her fists against the wall. But, she reminded herself, as the cold reality began to seep through her hurt and fury, she had a flight to work. This was no time for hysterics.

Robbie stood up, went over to the washstand, and glanced at her white, pinched face. The effort not to cry was tremendous. Her throat ached with distress. Determinedly she took several long breaths until her pulse quieted and her head stopped pounding. She ran cold water over her wrists, soaked a paper towel, wrung it out, and then applied it to her forehead and eyes.

She still had a good half hour before her plane took off for Atlanta. *Just time enough,* she decided.

There was a desk in the lounge with writing materials and intercompany envelopes. Quickly she sat down and scribbled a note, put it in an envelope, and, before sealing it, took the little key out of her uniform pocket, dropped it inside, and pressed the flap shut.

Holding her head high, she straightened her slim shoulders and walked back into the main lobby and over to the Trans-Continent ticket counters. Behind it was a slot marked "Intercompany Correspondence." Robbie dropped the envelope in the slot. She knew Tyler would find it in his mailbox in the pilots' lounge tomorrow.

With that, she turned and walked resolutely toward the departure gates, to board her flight back to Atlanta.

Tomorrow she would call Kara Collins, the Chief Stewardess, and tell her that she had decided to *accept* the promotion job and go on the public relations tour for Trans-Continent. She needed desperately to get away and have a total change. If she kept on flying her regular schedule, she ran the risk of running into Tyler again. She could not face that or the constant threat of hearing about his latest girlfriends.

Yes, Robbie assured herself, *sometimes the bravest thing to do is run and never look back.*

Chapter Seventeen

"Well, after today, let's see what our schedule looks like—two more cities and ten more interviews. There's the Rotary Club luncheon, the Business and Professional Women's Banquet, the radio talk show tomorrow morning, then . . ."

Robbie held up her hand pleadingly. "Oh, Todd, spare me!" she begged.

"Had enough of being a celebrity, huh?"

Robbie sighed heavily and stirred her coffee thoughtfully. She and Todd Maynard, Trans-Continent's promotion and publicity agent, were having breakfast in the airport coffee shop in San Francisco. They had just taken the early-bird flight up from Los Angeles that morning after a hectic whirlwind of events there. The tour had been encouragingly successful but, now in its fifth week, Robbie was beginning to feel the strain.

"Well, you can have some time off here," Todd told her. "Take a couple of hours this afternoon. You could go shopping at Fisherman's Wharf. Or we could rent bicycles and tool around Golden Gate Park, if you'd like to get some fresh air and exercise," he suggested.

Robbie shook her head. Todd Maynard was a dear and had no idea how each of his suggestions drove a spike of remembered pain into her heart. It was just those sorts of things that Tyler had planned for them to do together if she had come to San Francisco. Of course, all that was over, in the past, and she did not want even to think of Tyler. Maybe it was being here in San Francisco for two days on the tour that was making her so edgy.

"What I probably need is a hot bath and a nap," Robbie said rather apologetically. "It gets tedious always trying to project the alert, energetic, smiling Trans-Continent stewardess image—especially on less than six hours sleep."

"I understand," Todd nodded sympathetically. "Well, as soon as we go to the hotel and do that one interview . . ."

Robbie did not really listen as Todd outlined the day's activities. Unconsciously her mind wandered to how different this, her first trip to San Francisco, was from the one she briefly had hoped to make. All the while, a running dialogue went on inside her head.

He never meant anything he said.

I never really thought he did.

But you were beginning to believe it! Come on! You were flattered.

Yes, but I was a fool. I should have known better. Right from the beginning I had told myself we had no future together. And he certainly made that clear enough.

Why couldn't she forget Tyler? Why was it so hard to get over someone she couldn't trust? *I should have known better!*

"Finished?" Todd was asking. Robbie blinked, coming slowly back into focus. "You've hardly touched your food," he said accusingly.

"No appetite. I'm too tired, I guess," she replied. They got up, and Todd went over to the cashier to pay their check. Robbie stood idly looking over the display of candies and chewing gums. Then she was startled to hear a voice that she would recognize anywhere call her name. Without turning around, she walked swiftly out of the restaurant into the terminal lobby. But she was not fast enough. She heard footsteps coming closer from behind her. Then strong hands gripped her arm and swung her around. Tyler was towering over her, his gray-blue eyes riveting on her. Robbie was momentarily shocked.

"Robbie, don't run away," T. J. pleaded. "I've got to talk to you. You have to explain that note you sent. Why have you refused to take my calls? I don't understand. . . ."

"There's nothing to understand. It should be clear. It's very simple. I'm not interested in any man who hands out keys to his apartment like prizes in a Cracker Jack box!" She wrenched herself free, feeling all the accumulated bitterness of the last few weeks well to the surface. Who did he think he was that she would come anytime to his beck and call? Her eyes flashed defiantly—while the sight of him tore her heart into ribbons.

Tyler dropped his hold on her and stared at her with a puzzled expression. "I don't know what you mean by that."

"Please don't take me for a complete idiot. Whatever you may think, I wasn't born yesterday."

Tyler started to say something but was interrupted by Todd Maynard, who came up to them and said half-jokingly, "Is this man bothering you, lady? Hi, Captain Lang. How're things going?"

Robbie took the opportunity to make her escape. "I'll see you at the hotel, Todd," she said coolly and walked quickly in the direction of the cabstand.

Two days later in Seattle, Todd regarded Robbie speculatively and remarked, "So, after the tour is over, what are you going to do?"

"You mean after I collapse?" She smiled ruefully.

"Yes, after that, and a week in the sun doing nothing."

"I don't know. I think I'm ready to make a drastic change of some kind," she said thoughtfully, toying with the mound of scrambled eggs on her plate which was fast getting cold and inedible.

"Have you ever thought of modeling as a career?" he asked.

"Modeling?" she raised her eyes, regarding him in surprise.

"That's what I said. You're not classically beautiful, but you've got great bone structure, dynamite eyes, and you photograph like a dream. I've seen the glossies of all the publicity stills that guy in Los Angeles took of you and, believe me, they are fantastic! Trans-Con is going to be ecstatic with them. They'll be using them for their own advertising. But you won't get anything from that. I think you ought to consider a career for yourself where you'll benefit from what you've got.

"I used to work in New York at a couple of pretty big agencies. I could give you introductions to the right people and recommend you to some of the top model agencies." He paused, giving her another professional once-over. "But, I guarantee, when those new Trans-Con posters come out with your picture, you probably won't *need* my help." He grinned. "You'll have it made."

"I've never thought of anything like that. I studied to become a nurse and then went into stewardess training. I thought when I stopped flying I'd go back to nursing and get some specialized graduate training."

"Well, you're still young. You've got your whole life ahead. You could model for a few years and save the money you make. Then you could do whatever else you want, live wherever you want. I'd give modeling some serious consideration if I were you, Robbie."

"Thanks for the vote of confidence, Todd. I'll think about it," she told him.

During the tour, she and Todd Maynard had become good friends. Personable, enthusiastic, ambitious, and with a cheerful, outgoing personality, Todd had been a great traveling companion. He was also happily married with two small children, about whom he was always bragging. That had given Robbie a nice feeling of security as the tour had progressed and their business relationship had developed into a comfortable friendship. She had come to trust his judgment and follow his advice on various aspects of the tour routine. He was considerate and careful not to over-schedule her, which she appreciated. In spite of their hectic pace, they had managed to slip away occasionally for a quiet meal, or to go to church, or just to walk in a city park. They had shared a lot of their thoughts, feelings, and Christian viewpoints in these times. Although Robbie had never told Todd about her heartbreaking romance with Tyler, he had sensed that she was at a crucial crossroad in her life.

It was nearly ten o'clock that night before Robbie finally got to her motel room. Her nonstop day had included a call-in radio talk show and a Jaycees dinner, with a long evening of after dinner speeches and some award presentations.

Maybe Todd was right. Anything would be easier than this, even the strenuous life of a model! At least, a good night's sleep is a job requirement for modeling.

She kicked off her pumps, took off her uniform, and lay down on the bed. She was physically tired and emotionally drained, grateful that Seattle was the last city on the rigorous tour. In the morning they would fly back to Atlanta, and tomorrow night she would be in her own apartment, in her own bed.

Robbie dragged herself up and into the bathroom to take a shower. Afterwards she wearily pulled down the covers and got into bed with a deep sigh of relief. She could not remember when she had felt this worn out.

But, tired as she was, sleep stubbornly evaded her. For some reason she tossed restlessly, unable to drift off. In the virtually soundproof room, the city traffic noises were dulled, but, somewhere in the distance, a siren shrieked in the night. *An ambulance? A police car? A fire engine?* Involuntarily Robbie shivered and whispered a prayer. She had been taught as a child in Sunday school to pray whenever she heard that sound. Someone somewhere was in trouble.

Strange, how things like that stay with you, Robbie thought. Lately, she had felt removed from all the old familiar things. On the tour, everything was so rushed that she never seemed to have a minute to herself, never any time for private devotions, sometimes not even a chance to go to church on Sunday. She had promised herself that, once she got back to Atlanta, she was going to get it together and figure out what the Lord wanted her to do with the rest of her life.

Finally, frustrated by not getting to sleep easily, Robbie sat up and turned on the light. She was too tired to read so she decided to watch some television. Maybe there was a good old movie on that she could watch until she felt sleepy.

Now, Voyager was already in progress when she switched on the TV set. Robbie had seen it a couple of years ago, but the plot line was romantic and distracting. Robbie slid further down against the pillows. Her eyelids had begun to feel heavy when, in the middle of a scene, a news bulletin flashed on.

We interrupt this program to bring you a special bulletin. A Trans-Continent jetliner with eighty-seven passengers aboard was hijacked shortly after takeoff from Omaha en route to San Francisco earlier this evening. There was only a cryptic report to the tower from the plane's captain, T. J. Lang, that a man had broken into the cockpit and was holding the pilot and copilot at gunpoint, ordering them to take the plane to Canada. Stay tuned to Channel 14 for news of any further developments.

Robbie jolted upright, horrified. "Oh, dear God!" she gasped.

She threw back the covers and fell to her knees and began to pray as she had never prayed before. Any hijacking brought special terror to airline employees.

She felt numb and terrified as she stammered out words, sending up desperate pleas in disjointed phrases. Knowing that she would have to get her thoughts in order—that she needed to pray with conviction, with assurance, with true faith, to be effective—she got up and went to the drawer of the bedside table, opened it, and took out the Bible she knew would be there.

Her fingers fumbled to find Psalms. Reading one of the ancient prayers that had calmed fears for thousands of years would help to put her own prayers in perspective. She found Psalm 91 and began to read parts of it softly out loud.

Surely He shall deliver you. . . .
His truth shall be your shield. . . .
You shall not be afraid of the terror by night. . . .
No evil shall befall you . . .
For He shall give His angels charge over you,
To keep you . . .

As she read the words her heart slowed to a normal beat, and she remembered how often she had been told that the Word itself has power.

She kept reading, turning the pages to Psalm after Psalm. She read ones that were her favorites and others that seemed particularly appropriate. The ones of David when he was fleeing for his life, in danger from Saul, were especially meaningful now.

She had turned off the sound of the TV set, just glancing at the screen occasionally to see if another news bulletin had broken into the program. Every so often she would get up from the bed and turn the dial to see if she could get any more news on any of the other Seattle stations.

She lost track of time. She just kept praying for God's help and for the hijacker, as well as for the safety of the passengers and crew. And Robbie prayed that somehow Tyler could bring the plane in safely without any injuries or loss of life.

Robbie thought of a prayer that her mother had sent her when she first had started flying. She took it out of her billfold, where she always kept it, and repeated it for Tyler.

The Light of God surrounds me;
The Love of God enfolds me;
The Power of God protects me;
The Presence of God watches over me.
Wherever I am, God is.

How I wish Tyler really knew the Lord, Robbie mourned. That was one subject which they never had talked much about. Sometimes, when Tyler had been at her apartment waiting for her so that they could go somewhere, he would pick up a church bulletin from the kitchen counter or idly flip through the Christian magazine she subscribed to, but he never had commented or asked any questions. Of course, she realized that had been one of her big mistakes. She had never really brought up anything they might disagree on.

Not that it mattered anymore. At least not for *her* sake. She realized it was for *him* that she wanted a real relationship to God. If he had that *now*, in his moment of extreme danger, he would be safe and secure—no matter *what* happened.

Robbie didn't know just how long she had been waiting when she saw the "Special Bulletin" logo flash onto the TV screen. She quickly turned up the sound.

> The hijacked Trans-Continent jetliner is safely on the ground in San Francisco. Channel 14 has learned that the gunman was successfully subdued and is now in the custody of police and airport officials. No one was injured, and the deplaning passengers were unanimous in their praise of the bravery of the plane's captain, T. J. Lang, in disarming the hijacker, aided by the copilot and flight engineer, and for the cool performance of the rest of the crew members in this emergency. In just a minute we will bring you an exclusive interview with the courageous Captain Lang.

A few seconds later, she saw Tyler's face, a little haggard, eyes dark-circled with fatigue, but with the familiar sparkle lurking in them in spite of the ordeal he had just been through. Articulately and calmly, he reported the sequence of events of silent communication in the cockpit, quick action, and cooperation of his copilot and engineer in wrestling the gun from the hijacker and subduing him. T. J. fielded questions and lavished compliments on his fellow crew members and the passengers.

The interview ended and, as Robbie reached out to turn off the set, tears were streaming down her cheeks. The long nightmare was over.

Thank God! she breathed gratefully.

Chapter Eighteen

With the publicity tour over, Robbie came home to find that she had missed Atlanta's beautiful spring. As she drove home from the airport, she was disappointed that, all along her street, the dogwoods and azaleas were finished blooming.

But to her delight, she found in her own yard the grape hyacinths and the plants the nurseryman called "sweeties" blooming in lovely lavender and yellow harmony. Robbie smiled, remembering the old man's words when she had bought them: "Mebbe, if the Lord loves you, they'll bloom together."

Cyrano was on the porch railing blinking in the sun when she came up the stairs. At first he ignored her, as if letting her know that he was not about to greet her with much enthusiasm. But when Robbie left the front door open to admit the warm weather, Cyrano soon meandered inside, meowing for attention.

Robbie picked him up. Cuddling him in her arms, she listened for his inner engine to start the purring as she stroked him. It gave her spirits a badly needed lift.

Among the accumulation of a month's mail Robbie found a note from Martie Evans that gave her a twinge of conscience and a twist of the old knife of pain in the wound that Tyler had made. Martie's letter read in part,

Hi, friend. What gives? Have you eloped with your dream pilot and gone away to float on Cloud Nine, or what? I haven't heard from you in ages. Let me know what's happening, okay?

Love always, Martie

Robbie had not had the courage to write or call Martie. The scars had not yet healed, and somehow she had not been able to talk to *anyone* about Tyler, not even someone as close and dear as Martie.

Robbie knew she was depleted in many ways. The physical toll of the strenuous tour, climaxed by the severe emotional trauma of the night of the hijacking, had lowered her energy level badly. She had asked for and been granted two weeks of R and R from the airlines.

While the two weeks of rest did help Robbie recover from the extraordinary demands of the tour, her real battle in the days that followed was fighting the residue of hurt and resentment left by what she considered to be Tyler's betrayal.

She discovered that getting over a broken relationship is hard work. She also learned from her struggle how deep her feelings for Tyler really were. Even after she had given up some of the anger, it had been replaced with a kind of aching sadness. Something precious had gone out of her life—forever. But there was a long period of emptiness to fill up. With *what*? That was the problem.

As she returned to her regular work routine, there were still other hurdles to get past. She tried having a few dates, but found herself restless and bored on most of them. Often she wished she were home reading instead. She tried making a list of things to do on her days off. She went through a stream of ambitious plans and brief enthusiasms, such as growing her own herbs in little pots on her kitchen windowsill and using them in gourmet recipes, attending a jazzercise class, taking tennis lessons, and having her colors done. She weeded out deadwood from her wardrobe and then promptly lost interest in clothes. It all seemed pointless and a waste of time. She began to see her activities as self-indulgent and longed to put some purpose back into her life. She always came back to the question, *What does God want for me? What is out there in the world for me to do?*

During this bleak time Robbie began making weekly long distance calls home. It somehow eased the loneliness she was experiencing just then. Talking to her mother, dad, younger sister, and brother about the trivial, inconsequential, everyday sorts of things that were happening at home helped to make her feel less abandoned. Robbie realized she had been so focused on her relationship with Tyler that almost everything else had taken second place in her life. Even though her phone bill multiplied, her sense of belonging and important values was renewed.

She began to consider seriously the possibility of quitting the airlines altogether, taking some refresher courses in nursing, and getting her graduate degree. Maybe she even would go overseas, eventually, as a medical missionary. She had considered that once. Wouldn't that be more worthwhile than what she was doing now?

She had never meant to go on flying indefinitely, anyway. After three years, the thrill and glitter of the job had long since worn off for her. She had harbored the dream briefly that when she left, it would be for her marriage to Tyler. Now that dream was ended.

What does flying hold anymore for me? Roblynn demanded.

What did she even have to show for the last three years? A small gold Million Mile pin on her uniform lapel—that was all. Roblynn smiled wistfully.

Robbie knew stewardesses who had gone on and on, addicted to the lifestyle. Girls who loved buying their shoes in Rome, their sweaters in Scotland, their lingerie in France, and who spoke casually of lunching in Paris and dining in London. She did not want to become a professional fly-gal. It became too hard for them to adjust to earthbound jobs or even marriage. Girls who flew too long never seemed to be able to settle for everyday life.

As she thought back over her life to this point, Robbie remembered the Christian camp she had attended the summer she was sixteen, after her junior year in high school. She had been very much aware of making some decisions about college and a career. At the last campfire, a talk by the head counselor had impressed her strongly. He had urged them to seek God's plan for their lives and to let Him use all the natural abilities and talents that He had given them.

She had brought home from camp that year a poster and put it on the wall in her room, where it had remained all during her senior year. The poster was dominated by a large colorful sunflower and the saying, "BLOOM WHERE YOU ARE PLANTED."

I ought to be able to be a blessing on flight as well as anywhere, Robbie decided. *I don't have to make any huge change—not right away anyhow. Just by being the best me I can be—I can be a witness while flying, with other members of the crew and serving my passengers. It doesn't matter where you are—just who you are and what you stand for. That's what counts!*

That conclusion took some of the pressure off Robbie. She began to relax, to work her flights with a new enthusiasm, and to look for possibilities for God to work through her.

Even though her work life improved, her personal life remained stale and flat. On her days off, she took to haunting antique shops or prowling through secondhand stores. In one, where the sign outside promised, "WE BUY JUNQUE AND SELL ANTEEKS," she found an old chest of drawers. It had about ten coats of paint on it, but the store's owner told her that it was good birdseye maple underneath and showed her where he had peeled away the layers of paint to the wood. She bought it, took it home in the trunk of her little car, and hauled it up to the apartment. There it sat for days.

She had purchased all the materials necessary to strip, sand, and stain the thing, as well as the tools and the plastic drop cloth to protect the floor. But somehow she could not get the impetus to start on it.

Every time she came in from a flight, there it was, mocking her. One night, she could stand the sight of it no longer. The chest reminded her so blatantly of how she had let her broken dreams depress her and stifle her energy.

Even though it was after eleven at night, she slapped on the paint remover, opened all the windows to let out the harsh odor, changed into jeans and an old T-shirt, and then started scraping. It was 4 A.M. when she finally quit.

As the little chest began to take on a lovely mellow luster and finally was set in place between the two front windows in the small living room, Robbie took enormous pride in her accomplishment. The task had proved to be a catharsis. She even hung the lovely Bermuda watercolor over the chest and felt only a kind of lingering regret over what might have been.

The brief lovely spring exploded into summer, and summer into an autumn of brilliant, sunny days alive with fall's vibrant colors. But, with the beginning of October, Robbie began to experience an indefinable melancholy. She did not realize that her forlorn feelings were the legacy of sadness lingering from her shattered romance.

Driving home after her flight in an early dusk toward the end of the month, Robbie recalled with amusement a conversation she had overheard between two of her passengers after the end of the movie they had just finished viewing on board. Recently Trans-Continent had been showing *Gone With the Wind* on its Atlanta-bound flights. As Robbie had come down the aisle checking seat belts, she had heard a young man saying to his wife, "You women always think Scarlett is going to get Rhett back. But I've got news for you—*it isn't going to happen*. Scarlett *isn't* going to get him back!"

Robbie laughed a little now, just thinking about what had been said. The man had been so emphatic! Maybe he was right. Maybe many women lived on fantasy. *Maybe it was Scarlett's fantasy that she would get Rhett back, and, most of us women believed she would. But real life is not like fantasy*, Robbie reminded herself. Not all her dreams or fantasies would bring Tyler back or change the things that had happened between them. It was time she got on with her life. Maybe the best thing, after all, would be to get out of the airlines completely and away from everything that reminded her of him and from the possibility of more chance meetings that just kept all her bruises from healing. Even her little apartment still had too many memories of happy times they had spent there together.

Cyrano was waiting for her in his usual place. Robbie picked him up, nuzzling her face into his thick fur and rubbing him behind his ears until the small purring sound deep in his throat indicated his pleasure. *It is comforting to have something glad to see me, if not someone,* Robbie thought ruefully. She remembered how Tyler had said *he* hated coming into an empty, silent apartment.

After she had showered and shampooed and put moisturizer on her face, Robbie wrapped herself in her old chenille robe, which was as soft and warm as Linus's security blanket in the "Peanuts" cartoons and which probably served the same purpose for her. Although not particularly hungry, she opened a can of clam chowder for herself and a can of tuna for Cyrano, who had followed her into the kitchen. As she got out a saucepan, her mind was still occupied with plans to put in for six weeks' leave to go somewhere and think about what her next step should be. Maybe she could go to her family's cabin at the lake near their home. It was still warm enough, and there was a wood stove for heat on chilly nights.

The persistent buzz of her doorbell intercepted her concentration. *Who could that be?* she frowned. Then she concluded that it was probably the paperboy who had come to collect. He lived in the neighborhood and watched for her car on collection nights.

She got out her billfold. Calling "Just a minute, Bart," she shuffled in her woolly slippers to the front door. Opening it, she gasped in total amazement.

"You!"

Tyler Lang smiled a tentative grin, one eyebrow raised. "I'm not Bart. May I come in?" he asked.

For a stunned moment, Robbie felt a traitorous hope spring up within her, but she quickly put it down. "What are you doing *here*?" she stammered. "I mean, in Atlanta?"

He looked handsomely casual in a gray turtleneck sweater, blue corduroy jacket, and gray slacks. "If you'll invite me in, I'll tell you all about it," he suggested.

"Well—" Robbie began doubtfully, then became conscious of her appearance. "I just—" She tightened the belt of her robe and made an ineffectual stab at her wet hair.

"I won't tell anyone this is the same beautiful girl I've seen smiling out from all those Trans-Con posters plastered on the walls of every airport from California east," he vowed with the old teasing quality in his voice that she remembered so well. "Please, Robbie, may I come in? We've got lots to talk about."

With inner reluctance and some mental reservations, Robbie opened the door wider and stepped back so that Tyler could walk inside.

"I just got in off flight. I'm making some coffee. Would you like some?" Robbie realized she was talking rapidly, covering her nervousness. Meanwhile, she led the way through the living room into the tiny kitchen and went behind the counter. She somehow felt safer with the divider between her and Tyler. "You sure you don't want some?" She held up the coffeepot.

"No thanks. Actually I'm coffeed-out. I drank about a half dozen cups getting up my courage to come over here."

"I have some decaffeinated," she offered weakly, then realized how stupid that must have sounded. But she

176

was surprised at the usually calm, self-composed Tyler admitting a need for courage.

The silence between them lengthened and grew awkward. Feeling shaky, Robbie grasped the edge of the formica counter for support. *Why has he come?*

Tyler walked around the small living room, his hands jammed into his pockets. He paused in front of the Bermuda watercolor and stood looking at it for a long moment. "I remember the day you bought this," he said quietly. "In fact, I remember *everything* about that trip to Bermuda."

Tyler came back over to the counter, folded his arms, and leaned forward saying, "Robbie, is there any chance, any chance at all, for us?"

Automatically Robbie backed up a little and reached behind her to steady herself on one of the kitchen chairs. Reminding herself that Tyler was all wrong for her and that he had betrayed her trust and disappointed and disillusioned her, Robbie wanted to clap her hands over her ears and not listen to whatever he had to say. She did not want to fall under his spell again. But her heart demanded insistently that she hear what he had come to say.

"First of all, I want you to know I've *waited* all these months to come. I wanted to test myself and be sure I wasn't on some kind of emotional high. That what I felt was *real*. I've waited since the hijack to come, mainly because I didn't want you to think I was trying to manipulate you or kid myself, or that I'd had some kind of deathbed conversion or anything like that. I wanted to test what I was experiencing and see if it would wear off. Well, it hasn't. And I think it's genuine. So I had to come.

"Robbie, I want you to marry me. Yes, I said, *marry*. I've never gotten you out of my mind. I tried to. Believe me, I tried, but I couldn't. Then, that night, the night of the hijack—you've heard how people who are drowning see their whole lives pass in front of them? That's something like what happened to me with that gun pointed at my head. I saw everything and realized I had nothing. Material things, plenty—a plush apartment with a fabulous view, a sportscar, a sailboat, money, freedom— they all spelled loneliness—a big zero! I knew there was a big hole in my life. Part of it was that I didn't have what you have, what I'd seen in you and secretly envied. A sureness, some strong convictions about life and its meaning and purpose."

T. J. shrugged. "Call it faith. Whatever it was, I didn't have it, and I knew I needed it—desperately. I thought I had a pretty good life going, but that night, I knew if I died that I'd have left nothing, no one. What I'd been missing all those months, Robbie, was *you*—what you had offered me and I'd been too selfish to take. Not just a fleeting affair, but a lifetime together of loving and sharing and building something worthwhile. I promised myself that, if I got out of that jam, I'd find out what I was lacking, go after it, and take some definite steps to make a new beginning. That's why I'm here, Robbie. I know now that I need you to show me how to believe like you do. How about it? Can you forgive me? Give me a second chance?

"Believe it or not, I'm even going to that church on Peachtree Street when I'm in town on Sundays—you know, the one on the bulletins you used to have lying around here. That minister makes a lot of sense. I'm even thinking about joining it. Someday."

"You mean here in Atlanta?" Robbie asked, bewildered.

"Yes. Didn't I say I've transferred back here . . . three weeks ago." Tyler grinned. "You've heard the saying, 'you can take the boy out of the South, but you can't take the South out of the boy.' I found I missed too many things. The thing I missed most was *you*, Robbie."

Still not quite able to grasp all that Tyler was saying, she asked, "What about the fabulous apartment with a bay view?"

"Swapping it."

"For what?"

"What would you say to a Cape Cod cottage, with a picket fence, and an old-fashioned garden?"

Robbie stared at Tyler blankly.

He walked around the counter and said softly, "I'd like to make a suggestion, Miss Mallory, about your future."

"What kind of suggestion?" Robbie asked dazedly.

"Marry me."

"I thought you weren't interested in marriage. If I remember correctly, you made that pretty clear. You said you liked being single."

"That was then; this is now. A guy can change. People do change, you know. Please believe me, Robbie, *I have changed.* I know what I want now. And I want you."

Robbie stared at him. Did she dare believe what he was saying? For a moment, her eyes moved over his face searchingly. Behind that teasing twinkle and under the slightly mocking smile, she saw the honesty, the yearning, and the tenderness that she had longed to see there. Inside, her heart began to melt.

But something held her back. She remembered that terrible day in Chicago when Sue Thompson had revealed Tyler's double-dealing. She would have to confront Tyler with that or it would always be between them. The key to his apartment which he had given to Sue would have to be explained, as well as her enigmatic remark. Stumbling for words, Robbie told Tyler about the meeting, what had happened, and what she had inferred from it.

He frowned. "Sue Thompson?" He seemed deeply puzzled, but gradually his face cleared. "You mean Ron Jamison's girl? So that's it!" Tyler's expression underwent a change until it was one of combined bewilderment and relief. "So *that's* what your note was all about when you returned the key! And what you meant with that crack about my handing out keys to my apartment like prizes in Cracker Jack boxes. I didn't understand *any* of it, until right now. Actually, Sue and Ron were secretly married but were waiting to announce it until Ron made captain and she could transfer her base to the West Coast. I lent them my apartment for a three-day honeymoon while I was out of town on that flight for four days."

He halted and demanded, "Now does that satisfy you? Are all your doubts cleared up, *and now* do I get my answer?"

Suddenly Robbie was in total confusion. Everything had happened so fast she was trying to make some sense of it. Distractedly she put her hands up to her face and hair.

"Oh, this is *awful*! This isn't the way a girl is supposed to look when she's being proposed to!"

T. J. threw back his head and laughed. Then he said, "You look just fine to me. Haven't you heard the saying, 'Beauty is in the eye of the beholder'? Robbie, it's always been your inner beauty that dazzled and attracted me. Don't you know that's all that counts?"

Utterly speechless, she made another ineffectual little gesture with her hands. T. J. roared and pulled her into his arms, hugging her tightly. "You little idiot," he said with rough tenderness. "Don't you know I adore you?"

She held her head back so that she could look up at him and asked, "You do? Really?"

"Yes, of course. Didn't you know? I've loved you a long time, and I don't intend to stop."

Foolish tears filled Robbie's eyes. Tyler brushed back her hair and wiped away the tears with his thumbs. Then he cupped her face in both hands and said very gently, "I guess there's nothing to do with a face like this but kiss it." He proceeded to do that very thoroughly.

A deep peace began to flow through Robbie. A happiness she had not dreamed possible filled her. Then she thought of the verse she had taken from the Christmas tree on New Year's Eve and taped to the kitchen bulletin board for this year. As the words came to mind, she realized joyously that they were being confirmed completely.

"Trust in the LORD, and do good; . . . And He shall give you the desires of your heart."